Final DANCE

Book 5 of the Lovers Dance Series

---

by Deanna Roy

Six-Time *USA Today* bestselling author of
The Forever Series
The Lovers Dance Series

Sign up to be notified about new releases via email or text.

Casey Shay Press
PO Box 160116
Austin, TX 78716
www.caseyshaypress.com

Paperback ISBN: 9781938150692

eBook version 1.0

Summary

Blitz and Livia plan their quiet wedding. But guess who has other plans? See the fight between Hollywood and our couple for the biggest wedding in television history.

But even when the battle is over, life has one more big surprise. Watch Blitz and Livia evolve into the couple they were always meant to be as the *Lovers Dance* series comes to a close

Get emails or texts from Deanna about her new releases:
Deanna's List

PART 1: WEDDING

Chapter One

B oobs are in the sky.

Two of them. Crudely drawn, of course. You can't get very accurate in airplane exhaust.

The boobs are definitely not mine.

Mine don't, well...*hang*. Not yet, anyway. Give it a few years.

Blitz steps out of the limo. "Some people will do anything for publicity." He turns to take my hand as I slide forward toward the door.

"Who did that?" I ask. I peer up at the sky. The little plane has finished its work and motors out of sight. In the parking lot, several crew members have stopped to look up at the pendulous boobs and take shots on their cell phones.

"No telling," Blitz says. He leads me to the back door of the studio building.

I haven't been here in ages, not since Mack Williams took over *Dance Blitz*, the TV show that Blitz used to host. But this week we're here in LA for rehearsals for the final episode of Mack's first season. The one where he will supposedly choose a partner.

I hope he does, because they've already started the search for a bachelor dancer for season five. Mack is right out. Unlike Blitz, he won't get a second season to try again.

A security guard opens the back door, speaking into his headset. He'll let people know we're here. It will be a whirlwind few days.

A tiny girl, barely five feet tall, approaches, also wearing a headset and cradling an iPad like a baby. "Blitz, Livia, so glad to see you. Let me get you to wardrobe."

"Jumping right in," Blitz says with a grin.

"Just like old times," I say.

I pause to look at the sky one more time, feeling some anxiety. Maybe the boobs aren't meant for us. Maybe it's a joke for some other show that is also filming right now. It could even be a publicity stunt for a strip club.

I shake it off as we walk into the building.

After practically living at this studio during the five episodes I shot with the three other finalists, it's strange to have been gone so long. Well over a year has passed. I've been a ballerina for an entire production of *Sleeping Beauty*, and several other offers have come my way since the release of the DVD version of the ballet.

I haven't taken any. Blitz hasn't accepted any long-term jobs either.

We've been planning our wedding. A small ceremony on a cruise ship. Just a few friends and family. It's a very exclusive cruise line, so we don't have to worry about spies or paparazzi.

Devon, the director of *Dance Blitz*, catches up with us as we're led down the hall. I smile inside, remembering how he tries to channel Steve Jobs with his black turtleneck and jeans. It's all he ever wears.

"Blitz, good to see you again. Livia." He nods at me. "Did you get the script of the show?"

"Nope," Blitz says.

Devon's expression gets hard. "I sent them to Hannah a week ago."

"I'm not speaking to my agent," Blitz says.

"Still? It's been a year," Devon says.

"I hold a grudge."

"All right. It's nothing much," Devon says, motioning us to follow him. "You have two dance numbers. One with Mack, followed by a little session where you give him some advice. Then one with Livia. Where you propose, of course."

"I what?" Blitz stops dead.

"You propose to Livia. You know that has to happen on camera, right? It's in your contract."

Nobody told us that.

Devon glances down at the engagement ring on my hand. "How many people have seen that?"

I clutch my hand to my chest. "We've kept it quiet."

"Any public appearances with it on? Any pictures?"

I shake my head. "Not that we've noticed."

Blitz proposed at a small recital at the dance academy where we train. A few of the parents who saw it might have posted something, but probably on private feeds.

"You would have known," Devon says. "Blitz going off the market would be big news."

"You forget," Blitz says. "We're out of the spotlight."

"Not for long," he says. "But if you're right, your proposal will seem real to everyone."

Blitz and I glance at each other. Of course it's real! We're getting married!

I'm about to protest when Amara, the show choreographer, pops her head out of a rehearsal room. "Finally! I need Blitz in with Mack as soon as you can spare him."

"I need them for wardrobe," the girl says.

"I'm briefing them on the storyline," Devon says.

Amara rolls her eyes. "Send Livia to wardrobe. Her gown is the issue. I'll take Blitz. Devon, you can fill him in during breaks."

Devon shakes his head. "You can see who wears the pants around here."

"Shut it," Amara says. "Or I'll send you out on camera without pants."

"Wouldn't be the first time," Devon says.

Blitz sighs and gives me a quick kiss. "I'll see you in a bit."

Then he disappears behind the door.

"This way," the girl says.

She hurries on down the hall, but I don't follow her just yet. I'm still stuck between the idea of a televised proposal and the lack of pants.

I stare at the door, then look down at my ring.

The girl stops and turns back. "You'll probably want to take that off before any of the cast sees it and tweets something. The producers will be pissed if word gets out before they're ready."

"It's our lives," I say. "Our engagement."

"Hardly," says a cold voice.

I whirl around. It's Hannah, Blitz's agent. She's standing down the hall all stark and skinny, like a coat rack.

I tense up. We haven't spoken to Hannah since she orchestrated a comeback for the three jilted finalists, the ones who lost their chance with Blitz when I stormed onto the finale of the show and claimed him for myself.

Blitz was justifiably angry that his agent involved them, sparking a lawsuit that caused us to do a shortened season three of the show.

I still won.

But I lost a lot in the process. My anonymity. My privacy.

And, almost, access to the little girl I gave up for adoption when I was fifteen.

"Where is wardrobe?" I ask the short woman. I don't want to talk to Hannah, especially without Blitz. She isn't my agent. I have no business with her.

And I hold grudges too.

The girl recognizes a fight, though, and doesn't move.

Hannah approaches, her heels ringing on the shiny floor. She's as stilted and perfect as always in an immaculate lime green pencil skirt and matching jacket. Her blond hair sweeps her face in a smooth bob.

"Livia," she says, "why don't we put that ring someplace safe until it's time for Blitz to give it to you on the air?" She reaches out a hand.

I turn away from her. "No."

"Be reasonable. Blitz's contract specifically states that in the event of an engagement to one of the finalists of the show, the proposal is the property of the franchise and will be aired exclusively by the network."

"It's my engagement," I say.

"You're under contract too," she says coldly.

I look at her then. "You don't manage me."

Hannah sighs. "I'll send someone to reason with you." She waves her hands airily. "But I wouldn't let anyone see it. I would hate for a breach of contract lawsuit to wipe out your earnings from the show." She starts walking down the hall, the sharp tap of her shoes starting up again.

I clasp my hand around the ring. "We already got engaged," I call after her. "You can't erase that it already happened."

Hannah laughs but doesn't turn around as she calls out, "If his millions of fans didn't see it, then it *didn't happen*."

She turns the corner and disappears.

"Great," I say.

"Nobody likes her," the girl says. "She's a pill to be around."

I gaze down at the ring. "You think I should hide it?"

"I've got a Band-Aid in my bag if you want to cover it."

"I'll put it on my necklace." I tug the ring off my finger and unclasp my necklace, sliding the ring along the chain. Once the necklace is back in place, I tuck the ring beneath my shirt.

I can't believe *Dance Blitz* has already taken over my life again.

Chapter Two

Wardrobe fits me into a pale blue dress, my signature color from the show. Kendra, the production stylist, comes to supervise the adjustments and choose shoes. The dress is rather nondescript, giving me no hint about the sort of dance we're going to do. Definitely not ballet, though. All the shoes have heels.

I pause at the makeup chairs to give a quick hug to Cecilia, a hairdresser who is dear to me after she helped me the first time I arrived on *Dance Blitz*, a shy, frightened nineteen-year-old about to storm onto live television.

"So glad you're still here," I tell her. Her spiky hair isn't blue anymore, but pink and green.

"It's not the same without you and Blitz around,"

she says, leaning against the back of the tall salon chair.

The other makeup and hair stylists crowd around as she fills me in about Mack and the more memorable dancers from this season.

"Any Giselles this time?" I ask. Giselle was one of the three finalists who made Blitz's life hell during season two and during our abbreviated rematch. A tweet about her nearly cost him his career.

I'm not entirely sure she isn't behind the boobs in the sky. It's the sort of thing she'd do.

"Two, in fact," Cecilia says. "But not as toxic, really. Just drama queens."

"We've been watching the episodes," I say. "But we've been totally out of the loop about what's going on behind the scenes."

"They really ramped up the bitchy behavior to try and stand out," Cecilia says. "It's not the same at all."

"I did notice more interaction between the contestants and fewer dance numbers," I say.

"Uh-huh, you got that right," one of the other stylists says. "It's like this isn't even a dance show anymore."

A pair of women enter the room, and the freeze coming off their attitudes is like a chill in the air. I recognize them as two of the current finalists, Dolly and Veronica.

"I'm not talking to you," Dolly says, as if they're

continuing a conversation. She is strikingly tall, with dark brown hair to her waist. "Save it for the cameras."

"Hey, Dolly," Cecilia says. "I've got my instructions for your hair. We're going to do a practice run on your style for the live show."

I step back as Dolly sits in the chair. She sees me, and her face changes completely. "Oh my God, it's Livia!" Her voice is sweet and false. "Does that mean Blitz is here?"

"He's rehearsing with Mack," I say, my guard going up immediately. What does she want with Blitz?

Veronica sits in another chair. She is extremely petite, barely five feet tall. Her blond hair is twisted in a bun and shows its dark roots.

She tilts her head at me. "I guess we'll be doing rehearsals with you?"

"I haven't seen the itinerary," I say.

"Are you doing a dance with her?" Veronica asks Dolly.

"I didn't see a number like that," Dolly says. Cecilia starts back combing her hair. "Ouch, take it easy!" She turns to give Cecilia a dark look.

Cecilia says nothing but waits a few moments before resuming her work.

"I'm Veronica," the blonde says, extending a hand. "It really is nice to meet you. Everyone talks about how you stormed the stage. Impressive move. You can't buy that sort of publicity."

I shake her hand. "I didn't do it for publicity."

Veronica shrugs her shoulders as if she expects me to say that. "Everyone has tried to do something similar, stomping on set during other dates, interrupting private conversations."

"They had to keep the filming schedule secret in the end," Dolly says. "I didn't do any of that nonsense."

"They eliminated those girls pretty fast," Veronica says. "I think Mack was upset they cut Felicity."

"Mack didn't cut her?" I had seen that tearful episode a couple weeks ago. She had been a fan favorite.

"She got the blue card," Veronica says.

Blitz told me about those. Anyone could report another contestant, and if enough people agreed, the bachelor had to cut her.

The girl who led me to wardrobe jumps from her seat in the corner, her iPad blinking black and white. "Livia, you're needed in rehearsal right now."

"Nice meeting you both," I say. "Good luck."

"Oh, Livia, I would just love it if I could get some pointers from you before the live show," Dolly says. Her voice has that syrupy quality again.

"Both of us," Veronica says. "We could use it."

I nod at them. "We'll see how the schedules go."

The two women glance at each other with something akin to annoyance and wave goodbye. I'm not sure I want to get either one alone. I don't have anything I could say to help them. I had no idea what I was doing.

Still don't.

And they're both good dancers. The quality of the performances gets better every season. The third finalist, Beth Ann, is a stunning ballerina. She's struggled with the contemporary numbers, same as I did. Even though the staff feel like the dance numbers have become secondary, they are still very prominent and the only part of the show I still enjoy.

The hall is busier now. A man I don't recognize pushes a rack of costumes down the hall. A cluster of former contestants turn the corner, all decked in white swan outfits, and let up a huge squeal when they see me.

"It's Livia!" they shout, and I'm surrounded, drawn into hugs, women holding my hands and lamenting their lack of cell phones for selfies.

"I have to get her to rehearsal," the girl says. I really need to get her name if she's going to be my assistant. I miss my last girl, Jessie. She got me through season three.

This one pushes through the group and leads me out. She's tougher, for sure. More aggressive.

I'm not sure why the other contestants are so

excited to see me. They're more famous than me right now. They've got reporters and cameras following their every move. I'm quietly in the background.

Although I guess once the live show airs, it will be wild again.

Especially if they insist Blitz proposes.

We enter one of the rehearsal studios, and I'm introduced to a new trainer, Vince.

"You'll be waltzing with Blitz," Vince says, starting the music to a sweeping classical piece. "Everyone wants you the way you were. You're like old Hollywood already."

Old at twenty-one. Crazy.

At least the dance will be easy.

We spend an hour moving through steps and turns and sweeps. There are several lifts, but after a year of grueling ballet, none of this is hard. It's more a matter of learning the choreography. I've come a long way.

Partway through, Blitz arrives and sweeps me up into his arms. "Dancing with another hot young thing already?" he says, kissing my neck.

"I am," I say, laughing as his rough whiskers tickle my skin.

"We'll run through it again," Vince says.

I forget how well Blitz and I move together until we've launched into the dance. Vince gives us commands, and even if we don't follow the moves exactly, we still dance fluidly with the music.

"You guys don't even need me," Vince says. "Amara might flip if you don't follow her plan, though."

"You got that right," Amara says. We haven't noticed her walk into the space. "That was lovely, but the show has a lot more snap to it now. We'll want to get those extra lifts back in there."

Even with Amara's nagging presence, I still enjoy the next hour with Blitz. It will be nice to do a number with him again. We don't dance together all the time like we used to. It's how we first got to know each other.

So maybe I've missed the show, a little.

It will be good for us.

Chapter Three

When we arrive at the studio again the next day, there's a new image in the sky.

There's no mistaking who this one is from.

It's a banana.

"This is never going to die," Blitz says with a sigh.

White lines form the outlines of the image. Blitz's bad tweet, the one about Giselle, said she ate him like a gorilla. Bananas became a common theme in the talk shows about the incident.

I hurry through the door and catch up with him. "You think Giselle is hiring the planes?"

"She's not even working as far as I know," he says. "I don't see her throwing money away on skywriting."

"Didn't she get on *Dancing with the Stars*?"

He shakes his head as we walk down the hall toward the rehearsal studio. "No. She forgot that her contract restricts her from any other dance show for three years."

"Ouch."

"Yeah."

"Wasn't she up for some other show? A drama?"

"Didn't get it," Blitz says, nodding at Vince, who waits for us inside the open door to the dance room. "She blew it when she stalked off my show."

I don't ask how he knows all this. If he's talked to her or if someone has filled him in.

The subject of Giselle is really better left alone.

Although I wonder why she put her boobs up there yesterday.

I don't want to know that either.

After an hour of warm-ups and a couple run-throughs, Amara fetches us to rehearse on the main stage so they can check camera placement.

Costume designers descend on us, pinning a tuxedo top to Blitz even as we're shown the boundaries of our number.

We don't have to dance ourselves. Vince and another girl do it for us, and a team tapes blue marks onto the stage where we're supposed to land our lifts. Apparently there will be puffs of smoke for each landing as if we're walking on clouds.

Cute.

And way more complicated than anything we've done before.

The music cuts off prematurely, but Vince keeps swinging the girl, talking us through the motions.

And lift and catch and sweep into a bend.

Devon steps up and says to Blitz, "This is where you'll look into her eyes and decide right then and there that she will be your wife."

I shake my head. It's so ridiculous. I'm not an actress. How am I supposed to react to a fake proposal?

Blitz and I stand to one side of the stage, watching. The wardrobe people finally slide the pinned costume off him and he's free to move.

"What's after that?" Blitz asks.

"You hold while the new set comes down," Devon says.

The music blasts back in, far too loud, and I instinctively cover my ears.

"New sound guy," Devon says. He turns to the sound booth high over the audience seating. "Get it right or get out of my production!"

Silhouettes scramble behind the glass.

Devon takes a small towel from his back pocket and touches it to his forehead. Sweat is beading along his skin. "Live show with a new sound designer. Jesus."

"What happened to the old one?" Blitz asks.

"Ran off with a semi-finalist," Devon says. "We

had to cut several people covering for them, too. The mixer is the only one who's still on."

"You couldn't wait until the end of the season?" I ask.

"Talk to the producers. They were the ones who did it," he says. He turns to the back of the stage. "Where's the rainbow?"

Blitz makes a gagging sound. "Rainbow?"

"It's your proposal set," Devon says. "It might be a little over the top."

A sheer scrim comes down, lit to be transparent so that you can see the scene behind it.

"And rainbow!" Devon calls.

The colors change, and the scrim becomes opaque. An iridescent rainbow slides across its surface, appearing slowly, as if the sun itself was creating it.

"That's beautiful," I say.

"Okay, I approve," Blitz says.

"The lighting girl is brilliant," Devon says. "Thank God for that."

I walk across the stage. Our stand-ins are still now, the dance done. I touch the scrim, and it wavers slightly. I'm always so amazed at the magic that can be done with lights.

Another wardrobe person arrives with my blue dress. She holds it against her body.

"Light test," Devon bellows. He hurries to one of

the cameras to view the scene as it will be broadcasted.

"All wrong!" he shouts. "That dress is too light! I said CERULEAN!"

The woman holding it rushes off the stage. I guess that will mean more fittings for me.

The music starts up again, and Vince and his partner begin dancing. I move out of their way and head back to the side.

Blitz hums along, then takes my hand, sweeping me into a tighter, less buoyant version of the dance.

Vince sees us and moves his partner aside to give us room. Blitz and I run through the dance, missing a couple lifts still, but generally getting it right. When we come to the dip, he gives me a silly grin. "Wanna get hitched?" he asks.

"Not until I see a rainbow," I say.

The scrim comes down.

"I like that," Devon says. "You insisting on a rainbow."

Blitz and I break out laughing, and he lifts me to stand up straight.

"Am I supposed to propose in a dip or get down on one knee?" he asks.

"Oh, a knee, for sure," Devon says. He gazes up at the scrim with the rainbow, fingers tapping against his thigh. "Yeah, we're going to do it. Livia, you will say, 'Not until I see a rainbow.' And Blitz will be all astonished, as if he isn't good enough. And then the rainbow will appear. Sheepish grin. Lift her up. Down on one knee."

"What about the ring?" Blitz asks.

"I've got it here," I say. I tug the necklace from beneath my shirt.

"A dancer will deliver it," Devon says. "At least that's the plan. The fantasy set makes it feel like the world was waiting for you to propose."

Blitz sighs. "Don't tell me. The dancer will be dressed like a unicorn."

"No," Devon says. "But that's not bad." He speaks into his headset.

Blitz groans. "We're going to be the worst meme ever to go viral."

"That's what they like," I say. "Free publicity. They'll make the GIF themselves and plant it."

He leans in close. "How about we just run away?"

"I'm in," I say.

A voice booms from over head. "We can hear that," it says.

Devon looks up. "Hear what?"

"Let's make a break for it," I say.

And we do, dashing off the stage, out the secure door, and into the hall. Our laughter echoes off the walls as we barrel down a corridor and turn to Blitz's dressing room.

We burst inside like hell is on our heels, and once

we're in the quiet, Blitz pulls me close for a long, lingering kiss.

Then we hear a throat clearing.

We break apart.

"You two are really something."

I turn. It's Mack Williams, the new dance bachelor.

"Oh, shit, I forgot this was your dressing room now," Blitz says.

"No prob, bro." Mack stands up leisurely from a stool near the big mirror. He extends a hand. "Good to see you again."

Blitz and Mack shake. He looks so different here than on camera, his hair calm rather than spiked and styled, his face stubbled instead of smooth.

"I don't think you've met Livia," Blitz says, turning to me. "Apparently I'm proposing to her on your show."

Mack's hand is gentle on mine. "That's what I hear." To me he says, "Sorry I missed you when we had the auditions last year."

"I was doing a ballet," I say. The whole process of choosing the new bachelor occurred while I was on tour. Blitz went up for it, but I was in Seattle.

"We have a ballerina this season too. She's a finalist," Mack says.

"I've seen her," I say. "She's very good."

"She didn't make any of the important troupes," he says.

I'm not sure how to respond to that. Beth Ann seems good enough compared to what I saw on tour. But many of the big companies only take dancers from their own schools.

I got lucky that a new corps formed around a Russian ballerina who defected to the U.S. I certainly could never have attended one of those ballet schools from age four. My family was way too poor to think about extras like dance lessons.

"Seems like the blonde is in the lead," Blitz says.

Mack settles back on the stool. "Yeah, hell of a thing, having it be a television vote now."

"You had a say in the final three, though, right? Or did they lie about that?"

Mack glances at the mirror. He shrugs. "They got rid of Felicity."

"Was she your pick?" I ask.

Both the men look at me and tilt their head toward the mirror.

Right, the cameras. That huge mirror hides at least three of them. No doubt at least one is always running, hoping to pick up something juicy.

"We should get a drink somewhere and talk," Mack says.

"Damn straight," Blitz says, clapping him on the back. "We'll get out of your space."

"I'm headed to rehearsal again anyway," Mack says. "But I wouldn't do anything crazy in here. This room is always hot."

"I forgot what it was like to be in a digital cage," Blitz says. "But you're nearly done."

"It's been a wild ride." Mack picks up a towel and slings it around his neck. "See you in rehearsal."

He heads out. Blitz takes a moment to look around. He stares at a bit of the wall for a moment and I wonder what's got his attention. I stand beside him, following his gaze. Then I see it. A muted red light behind the cover of a mounted lamp.

"They recorded the whole thing?" I ask.

"Looks like it," he says. He shakes his head and takes my arm. "Let's get out of here."

I couldn't agree more with that.

Chapter Four

M y new, deeper blue dress arrives the next day. Blitz's tux gets fitted.

New sky writing doesn't appear until afternoon. We hear about it from the staff.

Cecilia shows me the image on her phone. "It's that Giselle all right," she says.

This time it's a pig.

"They're getting fancier," another stylist says.

"Do they think Blitz will kiss the sky?" the wardrobe girl asks.

Blitz kissed a pig at a rodeo during the weeks he tried to repair his reputation after the bad tweet about Giselle.

I sit down to let Cecilia do a practice set on my hair. We have full dress rehearsal today.

"What do you think she wants?" I ask.

"She feels herself sinking into nothing," Cecilia says. "She wants to stay in the spotlight, no matter what it takes."

"The entertainment shows have caught on," says another girl. "They're all including the sky drawings in their segments on the upcoming finale."

"Great," Cecilia says. "Has Giselle spoken up?"

"She's acting all innocent," the girl says. "Insists it must be her fans."

"Ha, like anybody even remembers her," Cecilia says.

I shift on the chair. This whole situation makes me anxious.

But the day moves on. Blitz and I land all the lifts in the rehearsal, our last one since it's more critical that the finalists have the practice rooms and the attention of the trainers. This is all old hat and nobody's judging us.

I meet Beth Ann, the ballerina finalist. We're filmed practicing together in ballet gear, and I give her a few pointers. I want to apologize after, as she's been dancing since she was six years old. I'm only a few years into my own training.

But she's a sweet girl, probably too gentle for the debacle that is reality TV. I sort of hope she wins over Dolly or Veronica, although I'm not sure I wish this life on someone genuinely nice like her.

Devon likes our banter so well that he schedules

some quick spots with me and the other two finalists for optional footage should they need the time during the live show. After Giselle trounced off stage during our broadcast, creating a panic, they've learned to be prepared to insert emergency video clips.

I'm still not comfortable on camera, and the conversations with Dolly and Veronica are stilted and false. I doubt they'll get used.

The sky writing stops, and the day of the live show finally arrives. I start to breathe a little easier. I'm only involved in maybe five minutes of the entire hour, and then all this will be over.

We have to be at the studio ridiculously early for final rehearsals and wardrobe. Cecilia gives me a divine hairstyle reminiscent of my own season, a braided princess crown with a long fall of curls in the back.

Every time Blitz and I practiced the proposal, we made Devon sweat by changing it up. It's been a little joke between us to never do it quite the way the staff expects it. When Blitz and I are alone, we justify this because they're making us do this publicly when we already did it for ourselves.

A scant two hours prior to the live show, Hannah enters with a ring box. It seems my real ring, the one Blitz picked out for me, isn't showy enough for the producers. They're insisting Blitz propose with a ridiculous seventeen-carat princess diamond surrounded with pale blue stones to match my dress.

Blitz loses his mind, threatening to walk off the show entirely.

It's Mack who takes him aside and convinces him to follow along for now. After tonight, we're free of the show, and besides, the ring is just on loan. It's not like I have to wear it forever.

But even after the pep talk, Blitz has a gleam in his eye that I recognize. It's what prompted me to walk onto his own show finale two years ago. He's going to do something crazy.

So now I'm nervous.

He goes on stage for his dance with Mack. I watch it live from the wings, then head back to the dressing room to see the footage of Mack and Blitz talking about Mack's decision.

The swan girls are all inside, sitting on every surface, faces turned to the monitor.

"Livia!" they chorus when they see me.

One scoots over on a bench to make room. "Blitz is telling Mack to choose for love," she says, shifting her feathery headpiece. "It's so romantic."

I peer at the screen. The two of them are in the decision room. Photographs of Beth Ann, Dolly, and Veronica sit on a shelf.

"They totally stole that from *The Bachelor*," another girl says.

"Duh," comes from behind. "They've done it since the first season."

"Of both," someone else says.

I try to focus on the screen. Mack turns to Blitz. "I hear something special is happening for you tonight, bro!"

Blitz shrugs. "It's about time."

"You really going to propose right here on the show?"

"You know it!"

They clasp each other with a pound on the back.

Mack says in Blitz's ear, "Don't blow it."

I know he means not just the proposal, but the show itself. He knows how angry Blitz is about the whole thing.

They break for a commercial.

The door opens. Amara gestures for the swans to come out. "Positions, ladies!" she says.

They all scurry from the room. Amara glances at me. "I would go warm up with Vince," she says. "Your dance is in approximately fifteen minutes."

I nod. It will be more like thirty. The show has barely started. But it does go fast. I remember.

I stand up and turn to the mirror. My blue dress is brilliant and sparkles in the lights.

Sometimes when I'm all fixed up for a show or a publicity appearance, I see the new, more confident Livia. The one who charged onto a TV stage. Who left her parents' iron grip and made a life for herself. Who tried out and earned a spot in a national ballet tour.

I've held on to Blitz under incredible pressure that might have crushed a different couple.

But I lean in, and I know who is still there. Shy Livia. Scared Livia. The Livia who was told she was the shame of her family. The Livia who was locked in her home, unable to go anywhere. Who gambled on her first love and lost hard.

The Livia who gave up her baby for adoption.

Who didn't fight.

My eyes go wet, threatening my makeup. Cecilia and the staff will kill me if it isn't right.

I stand up straight. This is no time for thinking about the past. It's now, and Blitz is about to propose on camera. We'll get to share the thing we've kept to ourselves for months.

We're getting married.

I think ahead to the cruise. A private, exclusive boat. A few carefully chosen friends and family. No cameras. No interviews. No screaming fans.

Just us.

All I have to do to get there, is make it through the next half hour.

Chapter Five

✦✦✦

I watch from the wings as Barry Winston talks to the live audience during the commercial break. He's been the host for all four seasons, and he loves his job.

He wears his signature brown suit, his dark hair smooth and sleek.

Barry holds out his arms before the crowd. "We're just moments away from seeing Blitz and Livia together again on this stage! Are you ready?"

The crowd screams their excitement, and my belly calms. I forget that there are good moments in this business. This is one of them.

Blitz comes up behind me in his tux for the dance number.

"You ready for this?" he asks.

"We playing the proposal straight or winging it?" I ask.

"I say we do whatever the spirit moves us to do," he says.

I laugh. "Then I'm going to say, 'As long as a cheesy rainbow doesn't appear, I'll say yes.' That'll freak out the lighting staff."

Blitz grins. "Now that's my girl."

The countdown starts and Amara motions us to head out on stage. It's very dark, but we're still spotted by the live audience. They start screaming and chanting Blitz's name.

Barry speaks again, calming the noise. "Let's get ready to go live," he says. A hush falls over the audience.

The countdown clock begins, bright numbers on a screen beneath the sound booth. Ten, nine, eight.

I shift my gaze back to Blitz. We're in position for our dance number. Barry will introduce us, then the stage is ours.

The *Dance Blitz* theme song plays, then the spotlight comes up on Barry.

"Here it is, the moment you've been waiting for. The return of our original *Dance Blitz* bachelor, Blitz Craven, with the girl it took three seasons to find — Livia Mays."

The crowd cheers, and the lights reveal us. I smile

up at Blitz. I can't believe I'm doing this again. That I'm here.

The music begins, and we start our waltz. The first steps are easy and slow. I'm sure the entertainment shows will call it "classic Blitz and Livia" tomorrow.

But then it speeds up and the crowd responds, cheering as we go into our first lift, then a twist, then another lift. The first two cloud puffs don't go off, but I don't have time to think about it. We just keep dancing. We cross the stage, and when Blitz pushes me up and then brings me into a cradle, the third cloud machine *does* work. The audience goes nuts.

We spin and hit our marks, taking brief moments to catch each other's eyes when we can. My skirt whirls out, then settles, then catches air in another lift. Another cloud. Another cheer.

The song winds down, and we're breathing hard. It was a taxing dance. We hold our final position, and Blitz looks into my eyes.

And the magic is there. We don't have to fake it. He's missed this too, and he's loving that we're here together, on stage, in the world that brought us together.

Time feels suspended. His finger grazes my cheek, and he says, "Livia, you are the best thing to ever happen to me."

Cheers from the audience erupt but are quickly

shushed. Blitz waits them out. He's a pro. Then he says, "Do you think the whole world is waiting for me to ask you an important question?"

I laugh. "That sounds like Blitz Craven talking."

This is completely unscripted. I sense some tension in the wings. The rainbow scrim operator is probably panicking, wondering what to do.

"I think the world is with us," he says.

And that's when it drops. Behind us, the scrim lights up, a rainbow sliding across its surface.

"See?" Blitz says.

The crowd tries to erupt again, then hushes as Blitz lifts me out of the bend and gets down on one knee.

I watch the amusement playing across his face. What is he going to do?

"Livia Mays, I have a question for you," he says.

"You do, huh?" I say, trying to stop from giggling. The producers will be so mad if we muck this up.

"Would you be interested in a nontraditional domesticated arrangement?" he asks.

The unicorn dancer gallops across the stage, a ring nestled on her cloud pillow. Then she realizes what Blitz just said. She stops, looking around. She isn't sure if she's supposed to come out for that or not.

"You're totally messing this up," I say, sitting on his knee. "How about I give it a shot?"

Blitz lifts me up and stands. We face each other. "Okay. I'm game."

"Blitz Craven, dance god, teacher of wheelchair ballerinas, terrible driver, and secret French fry addict, I take you as you are. Will you do the same?"

Blitz turns me in slow circle. I lift my leg for a pretty arabesque, the skirt fluttering. It's the first move I ever taught him, the very first day we met. And no one knows that but us. Not the fans or the staff or anyone watching on television.

It makes this moment a little more ours.

Blitz continues the turn until I face him again, then says, "Livia, ballerina extraordinaire, talent beyond measure, brave stage-stomping girl, and stealer of blankets, I will take you as you are."

His hands go to my waist and lift me into the air. His palm shifts, and we're back into our language, the communication of touch and angles and movement. I wait a hairbreadth of a second, then roll down his arm, and his body, and he catches me in front of his hips, taking me into a dive, my face near the floor, feet in the air. It's a startling, fast move, like I'm falling.

The crowd gasps, then cheers.

Blitz sets me down and draws me close. "Will you marry me, Livia?"

"Only if you promise we will always dance."

His lips brush against mine. "I will."

The unicorn approaches, but we ignore her and her fake ring, spinning in alternating pirouettes across the stage. Confetti drops on both the stage and the crowd. The noise is tremendous.

We dance right into the wings, and the spotlight goes back on Barry. He will bridge the time gap between the proposal and the next commercial break, or lead into a video. Doesn't matter. Our time is done. The show is over for us.

Dancers and staff congratulate us as we make our way across the dark side stage to the exit door. Then we're in the hall, and the swan girls are hugging us. Wardrobe and makeup come out to squeeze us too.

We accept it all graciously. This is their chance to congratulate us since we got engaged far away and quietly.

The monitors blink for the end of the commercial and people start to scurry. There's one more number with the former contestants, and then Mack will announce his winner.

We head to the viewing room to watch with the producers. Everyone inside stands up to slap Blitz's back and shake my hand. They seem pleased with what we've done.

"That will be everywhere tomorrow," says Taya, one of the producers. "It was spot on for a big splash on the news shows." She is practically giddy, doing a little hip-shaking jig in her charcoal pantsuit.

"Glad to be of service," Blitz mumbles.

The door bursts open, and Duke comes in. "Hey, bud, getting hitched, I see!" he says. He's got his cowboy hat on, like we're still in San Antonio. He grew up there with Blitz and served as his bodyguard in LA. Now he works for Mack.

"I got this here back for you safe and sound," he says, passing something to Blitz.

It's my regular engagement ring.

"Thanks," Blitz takes my hand to slide it on. "The other one never even touched your skin," he says to me.

"Thank you for that," I say. I didn't really want to have to wear anything other than what Blitz picked out.

If the producers in the room are annoyed that we refused their audacious ring, they don't say anything.

Amara pops her head in. "Blitz, Livia, Devon has decided you guys should be on stage after the announcement of the winner."

"I thought we agreed we didn't want to upstage the new couple," Blitz says.

Amara's red mouth pinches into a sharp line. "We didn't really expect who the voters were going to pick. We think it's good if you're there to show support."

Blitz and I glance at each other, but we follow her. The other producers have stood up, anxious again.

I lean in to Blitz as we return to the dark wings of the stage. "I thought all the finalists were good," I whisper.

He shrugs. "I haven't heard any rumblings."

The big dance number ends. Barry leads to a commercial and the dancers scurry past. On stage, the crew sets up for the winner announcement. The three finalists arrive beside us, waiting for their cue to walk out. My mind flashes back to my own moment exactly like this one.

Dolly glances over and mouths, "Congratulations."

I nod back at her.

The backstage assistant moves the three finalists closer to the edge of the stage. Blitz and I hang back to make sure the lights don't fall on us and cause a distraction.

I spot Mack in the opposite wings, his arms waving wildly as he argues with Devon.

"Why does he know in advance?" I ask Blitz. "Isn't he supposed to find out when the rest of us do?"

Blitz shakes his head. "No. I knew."

"What?"

"They told me right before we went out. Remember how I just announced it?"

I recall that now. That I thought he might change it to whatever he wanted, even though there are T-shirts that will drop onto the live audience with the image of the winning couple.

"That's why they keep us separated. Mack is over there and the girls over here."

"It's a stressful moment," I say.

He turns to me then and slides his arm across my shoulders. "I always knew they would pick you," he says. "It wasn't in question."

"I don't think they should have told him," I say. "He's clearly upset."

"Probably they wanted him to have time to calm down. He wanted Felicity," Blitz says. "There was not going to be a good choice tonight."

"It sucks," I say. "Now he'll have to do publicity tours for months."

"Yep," Blitz says. "Part of the biz."

The countdown begins, and a stony-faced Mack heads out on stage.

"He can't pull himself together," Blitz says. "I'm going out." He lets go of me and heads across the stage.

I spot Devon with his headset in the opposite wing. His arms fly to his head, like he can't believe Blitz just strolled out.

The show has gone off the rails again.

Chapter Six

I squeeze my hands together as the countdown clock reaches zero. Blitz and Mack are talking intensely. Right as the theme song starts up, Blitz backs into the wings again, over near Devon.

I let out a sigh of relief and so do the girls. I can see from the tight set of their shoulders that they're anxious.

The spotlight falls on Barry, and he talks about the journey this season that led to the finale. There are clips of Mack with each girl. I can't see the screens backstage, but I can hear the audio.

I realize Felicity wasn't part of the swans. They didn't invite her back for the live finale. They must have feared she would do something. Or Mack would.

This business is hard, hard, hard. I wonder what Felicity will do next. She was a good dancer, more contemporary, best at jazz. I don't know what opportunities are out there for what she does.

I should convince Blitz to ask the other producers to nix that three-year non-compete clause. It's not fair to dancers who barely get by as it is. It should be six months at most. Or maybe end as soon as they're cut. Only the winner should be contractually obligated to anything other than maybe a nondisclosure agreement about what goes on behind the scenes.

Barry turns to Mack.

"Are you ready to find out your dance partner?" he asks.

Mack nods.

"Will there be a proposal tonight?" he asks.

To Mack's credit, he puts on his sly smile and says, "I guess we'll have to wait and see."

I let out a breath. He seems recovered. I'm not sure what Blitz said to him, but it seems like it helped.

"Let's bring the girls out!" Barry says, turning to our side of the stage.

Dolly, Veronica, and Beth Ann step out onto the stage. Dolly and Beth Ann join hands, but when Beth Ann tries to clasp with Veronica, she jerks her arm away.

The crowd notices and gasps.

Great. That's going to be an animated GIF meme within the hour. The one of me stomping on stage in season two has never fallen out of popularity. Occasionally I'll be out in public and some ten-year-old will see me and mimic my walk from the GIF.

Fame is a beast.

Beth Ann looks over at Dolly. She smiles and nods. They let go of their hands as well.

Mack has missed none of this, and his gaze flickers for a second. But this is live TV, and the show literally must go on.

Barry heads over to the girls and speaks with each of them to stretch out the suspense. Another countdown clock at the base of the stage lets him know how much time to spend on each segment.

Finally, he turns to Mack. "We've come to the moment for Mack to see his winner and let the world know who she is." He opens his jacket and pulls out an envelope.

Huh. This is new. They just had Blitz say it.

It's also fake. We all know that Mack has already been told.

That's show business.

Barry holds the envelope in the air. "This won't be a Miss Universe moment or a Best Picture mistake," he says. He waggles his eyebrows. "I already verified it myself."

I glance out at the audience, what little I can see due to the blinding lights facing the stage. Some lean forward, hands clenched. Others clutch each other. It amazes me, how caught up people can be about perfect strangers.

Barry walks over to Mack and hands him the envelope. "It's your lucky day," he tells him.

Mack nods and lifts the flap.

Barry moves to the edge of the stage, out of the light.

Dolly and Beth Ann instinctively hold hands again. Only Veronica stands alone.

The room is quiet as Mack pulls the card from the envelope. Then a slow drum roll begins, quickly picking up momentum. A cymbal roll adds a new pitch, increasing the tension. The sound people are on point.

Mack scans the crowd, drawing the moment out. I'm sure he practiced this over and over with Devon. He looks down at the card and does a little nod with his head. It looks like he is pleased, but we know better.

His gaze travels up and lands on the three women. He says in a level voice that betrays nothing, "The winner is Veronica."

Reactions are mixed. Some boos, lots of cheers. The screens flash on above the stage, casting a brighter light over the audience. I can't see what they say, but there's definitely a reaction, more mixed boos and cheers.

Mack picks up the flowers from the stand and

takes them to Veronica. Blitz stays back in his wings, so I stay in mine.

Dolly and Beth Ann are quickly escorted off stage by Barry.

The T-shirts drop, and while many of them are quickly grabbed, a few get tossed on stage. Amara pushes a couple stage hands out to fetch them.

There's supposed to be a final dance now, but I can see why Blitz and I were asked to be close, because everyone is unsettled. The boos start to outnumber the cheers, and more T-shirts land on the stage.

Blitz walks out, holding out his hands. Amara presses against my shoulder. "Go!" she says.

As I head out, I glance up at the video screens to see what got everyone so riled.

And there it is. The vote tallies.

VERONICA: 16,540,000
    Dolly: 16,539,942
    Beth Ann: 12,350,309

WOW. VERONICA WON BY BARELY 100 VOTES. OUT of millions.

And it's an oddly even number. Like it's been rounded up.

That does seem a little strange.

A chorus of "Dolly! Dolly! Dolly!" starts up.

More T-shirts land on the stage.

I glance at the wings. Devon is red-faced, speaking angrily into his headset.

Blitz takes my hand as we approach Mack and Veronica.

"Congratulations, you two," Blitz says, pouring on more charm than I've seen since his own dance show days. "Can I cut in?"

Blitz lets go of me and pulls Veronica into a quick whirl. The chanting stops. Mack takes my arm. "Looks like we're doing an unplanned dance."

My heart hammers.

Music comes on, fast-paced and upbeat. It's a foot-stomping, hand-clapping sort of song that engages everyone immediately. Soon the room is filled with a party atmosphere. The boos stop. No more T-shirts hit the stage.

Blitz links arms with Veronica and does a quick square-dance move. I see where he's going and do the same with Mack.

Blitz and I meet in the middle and we spin, then we're off again with Mack and Veronica.

The crowd stands to cheer, and the dance goes on. It's not what the show creators had planned, but the four of us are able to ham it up. We add feet kicking lifts and a few impressive twirls, making it up as we go along.

At some point more dancers filter in, and it's wild and loud with the four of us in the center.

Finally, the music gets a little softer and Barry talks over us. "Thanks everyone for being a part of the finale of Season Four of *Dance Blitz*! We'll be introducing our new dance bachelor very soon. Let's hear it for Blitz and Livia and Mack and Veronica!"

He threw us in there to avoid another round of boos.

Everyone's ready to live it up at this point, the shock worn off. The noise is deafening as we keep dancing through the chaos. When the countdown goes off and the cameras stop flashing, we continue a bit more for the live audience, then Blitz and I dance ourselves off stage.

The other former contestants keep going, linking arms and turning in circles, not wanting the moment to end. I glance behind to see where Mack and Veronica have gone. They smile and wave their way off stage, but the moment they're in the wings, they drop hands and immediately part.

"That's going to go well," Blitz mutters.

"At least we're not involved," I say.

We head back to the viewing room with the other producers. They're murmuring quietly and look up when Blitz and I enter.

"What do you make of this?" Taya asks. She's not dancing a jig now.

"Disaster," Blitz says. "Who authorized that vote count number? Nobody in their right mind believes the winner would have that many even zeros in the final count."

Taya exchanges a glance with Drake Addler, another of the producers who looks small and lost in his navy suit, his curly brown hair a riot over his bushy brows.

Blitz lets out an annoyed sigh. "Please tell me you did not fudge the numbers."

"I don't know who authorized that number on the board," Taya says after a pause. "But in a case where the vote is too close to call, we agreed that we would discuss the repercussions of each choice and make a decision."

"I was not part of that discussion," Blitz says.

"Lance, Drake, and I handled it," Taya says. "We had a majority and were unanimous."

Red creeps up from Drake's neckline. "Sorry, Blitz," he says. "Your vote wouldn't have mattered."

A couple women in the viewing room glance over at us, and Taya pulls Blitz over to the corner. He hangs on to my hand, so I go with him.

"Here's the thing," Taya says. "Dolly has a boyfriend who started threatening to talk to the tabloids after she was named a finalist. It was too late to blue card her. She couldn't win."

"What about Beth Ann?" I ask.

Taya shakes her head. "We should have taken her out early on. We really didn't need another ballerina. She was skating on Livia's fame. She wasn't what the franchise needed as we go into season five. We're barely holding our ratings position as it is."

"So you rigged it?" I ask. "You made Veronica the winner?"

"It was stupidly close already," Taya says. "It didn't really matter."

"And nobody thought to at least rough up the numbers?" Blitz says. "There were four bloody zeros on that tally. Anybody can see it was rigged."

I nod. "I'm sure Twitter is going nuts."

"We'll put out a statement," Taya says. "It will be forgotten in a week."

"Yeah, like Giselle," Blitz mutters.

"What do you mean by that?" Taya asks. "Is she back?"

"She's been skywriting over the studio," I say.

Taya waves her hand to dismiss the idea. "That's nothing. Talk to me when she does something people will actually notice."

With that, she waves at a man across the room and takes off. Drake glances over at us, taking another long swig of his drink.

"I guess in the end, it doesn't really impact us," I say.

Blitz shrugs. "If they plan to tank the show, I guess it doesn't." He rubs his eyes, and I wonder if he's thinking about all the money he paid to buy out Bennett as producer. It shouldn't matter. We have more than enough to live on in San Antonio, well, forever, as long as we're not stupid.

"We should go," I say. "Have a nice night in LA before we fly home."

Blitz takes my hand. "I hear you on that."

We walk out of the studio as the crew rushes around to clear everything. I glance anxiously up into the sky, but darkness has already fallen. No skywriting.

By this time tomorrow, *Dance Blitz* will be packed away for another season.

And we can live our lives in peace again.

Chapter Seven

We should have known better.

We've only been home a week when we find Danika waiting for us outside our practice studio, her spiky blue hair standing out against the gray walls. She's run the dance studio since it opened, built for her by her son-in-law Bennett. She has counseled me on more than one of my personal problems, and by the look on her face, it's about to happen again.

We let the wheelchair ballerinas take off with their mothers, including my biological daughter Gabriella with her adopted mother Gwen.

Gwen doesn't speak to us much, preferring to give us a quiet nod. She knows I'm Gabriella's birth mother, but we haven't told the little girl herself. I have to leave that to Gwen. She still feels very threatened by me. I must respect her wishes on this, because I have no legal claim to my daughter and only see her if Gwen allows it.

When the hall has cleared, Danika asks if we've checked our phones in the last hour.

"Nope. Totally focused on the girls," Blitz says.

"You might want to do that now," she says. "And please consider how you will arrive and leave the academy in the coming weeks. We really don't need more stalkers." She meets my gaze, and my eyes flit down.

I caused enough trouble already when my crazy ex, Gabriella's father, refused to leave the front of the academy and wound up getting arrested. We lost a lot of students during all that upheaval.

"It's that serious?" Blitz asks, pulling his phone from his bag.

He scrolls through his feed, his mouth turned down. "Great."

"What now?" I ask.

"They made a video. A damn video," he says.

Danika cuts her eyes down the hall to make sure no little ears heard Blitz.

"Sorry," he mumbles. "This is ridiculous."

"Just show me," I say.

He hits play. It's a *Dance Blitz* promo. Barry Winston fills the screen.

"*Dance Blitz* lovers, you all got to see the romantic

57

proposal between our original dance bachelor Blitz Craven and his winning contestant Livia Mays."

"I was never a contestant," I insist.

"Shhh, girl, let me hear!" a voice says.

I look up to see my friend Jacob standing tall and spectacular behind me. He teaches jazz to the boy dancers. He's rapt on the video. He's literally Blitz's biggest fan. He calls him his "impossible crush."

They play a clip of the proposal, then Barry comes back on.

"And now, you'll get to see it right here, their glorious wedding live on *Dance Blitz*." The camera pans out to reveal a lush garden with people setting up white chairs.

"What?" I exclaim. "We're not even there! Are they going to have lookalikes?"

"It's just for effect," Blitz says. "Look, the date is four weeks away."

A still shot showing the date and time of the live broadcast flashes up as the video ends.

"What?" I say again. "Who is engaged for four weeks?"

"Technically," Jacob says, "you got engaged at the spring recital."

We all turn to him with a frown.

"Just saying!" he says. "My auntie Carol married that good-for-nothing Doug after only knowing him a week. You got this."

"I don't have a dress," I say.

"Nobody has contacted me about this," Blitz says. "They can't go announcing that without our approval."

"Wouldn't that be your agent's job?" Danika asks.

Blitz and I look at each other. "Hannah," we both say.

"Have you gotten anything from her?" I ask.

"Her emails are auto deleted," he says. "Texts and calls have a silent alert and roll off the home screen automatically."

"Now that's some hard-core shade you're throwing right there," Jacob says.

"You better call her," I say. "Otherwise they'll roll cameras and we won't even be there."

"I'll have Shelly do it," Blitz says. "She's supposed to be running interference."

When Jacob looks confused, Blitz says, "My personal assistant when I'm shooting."

"Isn't she in Afghanistan?" I ask. "The women's caucus? Volunteering? That's why she wasn't at the live finale."

"Right," Blitz says. "Well, crap."

Little dancers flow around us as the next series of dance classes begin to fill.

"My point," Danika says, "is that if you're going to have a live wedding, or even if you're not, the press is going to follow you. Please draw them away from here."

"Will do, Big D," Blitz says. "If we have to take a break until it blows over, we will."

Danika nods. "Also, congratulations. I assume since all this is public, there will be a wedding soon, even if not the TV one?"

"We were planning to do it on a cruise," I say. I was also hoping Gwen could bring Gabrielle to be a flower girl. If it's a TV spectacle, we can't do that.

I seriously want to cry.

"Can they make us do this?" I ask.

"Of course not," Blitz says. "It's just a matter of what it will cost us to refuse."

"Is it like the proposal?" I ask. "Property of *Dance Blitz*?"

He frowns. "Yeah, I probably signed something foolish like that."

"I'll leave you two to sort it," Danika says. She takes Jacob's arm and drags him with her.

The parents settle on benches or hurry back to their cars for quick errands, the dancers all in their rooms. Thankfully they're all used to me and Blitz being around and aren't like the wild and crazy fans we encounter out in public.

I want to sit down and just weep that we're stuck. First the stressful short season where I had to compete for Blitz, then the live proposal.

And now this.

Chapter Eight

❧

Blitz tracks down Shelly, but with the time differences between Kabul and California, she can't easily get hold of Hannah. She tells Blitz he'll have to handle this part, but she'll be back for the "wedding."

Within a day of the announcement, Blitz and I have to abandon our house. It's fairly modest and tucked in a quiet neighborhood. Nobody's really followed us since we finished our *Dance Blitz* season. We haven't gated the property or worked to keep people away.

Up until now, all we had to contend with was the random paparazzi hanging out on the street trying to photograph us leaving. But our house is set pretty far back from the road, and our windows are well tinted. Blitz likes to zoom out and away so fast they can only get a few shots of the car itself before we're lost in the neighborhood maze.

It hasn't been a big deal.

But it is now.

We can barely get down our own street. Blitz immediately calls our driver and bodyguard Ted to bring a rental car, so we can make a dash inside for essentials.

After that, we leave Ted behind to watch the house while we hole up in a hotel. We can't go to the dance academy. We can't easily go out to eat or shop or anything. Blitz hires a second bodyguard, so we can leave Ted at the house and have someone else run errands for us.

Then somebody leaks our location, and the hotel gets flooded with fans. The manager assures us no one can get up to our locked floor, but we're totally stuck. I put on a scarf and sunglasses just to look down from the balcony and spot vendors selling Blitz and Livia T-shirts on the sidewalk below.

I've never seen anything like this.

On the third day of the madness, Blitz breaks down and calls his agent. He sets the speakerphone between us.

Hannah picks up on the first ring. "About time you called. You have the first planning meeting in three days. They want footage of a cake tasting. We have fourteen dresses arriving in less than a week for

Livia to try on. Everyone and their dog wants her to wear their design. People have been literally slaving to create something fresh for her."

"I don't get to choose my own dress?" I ask.

"Of course you do," Hannah says, her voice dripping with annoyance. "There are fourteen to choose from."

"What if I don't like any of them?" I ask.

"The winning designer will adjust it until you do," she says.

"Wait," Blitz says. "Did you green light this?"

"Of course I did," Hannah snaps. "This was always the plan. Have you forgotten how your original seasons were supposed to end? Before you went off-script? Contest. Choose girl. Meet parents. Propose. Engagement party. Planning. Wedding. Have you forgotten the two-million-dollar wedding bonus?"

"Right. Can't forget your percentage," Blitz says.

"Blitz," Hannah says sharply. "You got this gig because you were willing to sign over your wedding to the producers if you chose a contestant. If you hadn't signed that clause, there would have been some other hero of this story."

"I'm a producer now."

"That doesn't change your contract," Hannah shoots back. "You made this bed. Now lie in it."

"You want to film that too?" he shouts. "How about a honeymoon cam? Mount a lens right over the bed! What would THAT do for ratings?" His voice echoes off the hotel room walls.

"Don't be crass, Blitz," Hannah says. "It doesn't suit your new image. You are now a devoted future husband of the girl you found on your show, and you aim to marry her in full view of all the fans who voted her into your life."

"This is ridiculous," Blitz says. "I met her because you guys kicked me OFF my show, and I found her on my own, thank you very much." He moves his hand to jab the call button on the phone, but I stop him.

"Hannah," I ask. "What's the penalty for backing out?"

"Sixty-three million," she says coolly. "And that's only if I don't also sue him for my cut."

"Done," Blitz says.

"You think you can afford it, but once this happens, your share of the show will be worth virtually nothing," Hannah says. She pauses, and I picture her sharpening her claws.

"This is the same old threat," Blitz says. "We're tired of it."

"You danced with the devil. And now the devil is calling due." She lets out a long sigh. "Here's the thing. Nobody felt Mack's finale was good. The network is considering pulling out, canceling the show."

"What?" Blitz says. "It's a great show!"

"It's about to be a dead show."

"But I own part of it now."

I reach over and squeeze his arm. "Maybe we should let it go," I say.

He draws in a long breath. "So, they think the wedding will help save it?"

"Everybody loves a happy ending," Hannah says. "You guys seem to deliver."

"But it's our wedding," he says.

"It's still just a show. Do your real vows however you want. Imagine this is just an extended dance number."

"Are we dancing?" I ask.

"Of course," she says. "I have the treatment printed up right here. Should I forward it to you, perhaps, Livia? You do seem to be the more reasonable of the two, as hard as that is to believe."

"Yes," I say quickly. "But I want Jessie back on set with me."

"Jessie?"

"My assistant from season three," I say.

"All right," she says.

"And I'm going to vet my contract about the dress," I say. "I know I signed about additional shows, but I seriously doubt anyone put the dress in there directly. I'll hire my own lawyer for that." I'm already composing a message to Bennett in my head. He's

Danika's son-in-law and one of the few powerful people I trust even if he's not part of the show anymore.

Hannah sighs. "You'll love one of the dresses," she says.

"Just in case I don't," I say.

She sighs again. "Very well."

"We'll be in LA tomorrow night. Please let Duke know."

"If I can track that scoundrel down," Hannah says.

"Never mind," Blitz says. "I can find him."

"See you Thursday," I tell her.

Blitz aims his angry finger at the call button again and kills the connection.

"So you're on board?" he asks.

"You seem to want to save the show," I say. "I want what you want."

He stands and draws me up from my chair into his arms. "But it's our wedding."

"The wedding is just a day. It's the marriage that matters," I say.

He draws me close. "Livia, whatever did I do to deserve you?"

I laugh against his strong chest. "You learned to do an arabesque from a two-year ballet student and haven't let me down since."

He lifts my chin, his lips landing on mine. Everything relaxes in his kiss. The tension of the call. The shock of the possible cancelation of the show. The difficulty of dealing with his old agent.

It's just the two of us again.

Back in a hotel, like the early days, before we had a home.

Blitz has been my home for two years now. We've weathered a lot.

His fingers slide through my hair. It's long and tangled, and he works it smooth, his mouth still warm on mine.

The kiss deepens, and I let the world fall away. I hook my thumb in the belt loops of his jeans, reveling in the feel of his strong body against mine, his deft fingers working my hair.

"Shall we pretend there's a honeymoon cam above the bed?" he whispers against my mouth.

I sputter a laugh against his lips. "Blitz!"

"I could give them a show." He walks me backward across the hotel room until we're at the bed. His face turns up a moment. "Yes, it's right there pretending to be a sprinkler head." He waves.

He reaches around my back and slowly slides the zipper down the back of my pastel yellow sundress.

"Are we going for R or X ratings?" he asks me.

I shake my head. "You're terrible."

"Good. Triple X."

He runs his hands down my back. "Oh, no bra. The viewers are scandalized but titillated."

He pulls thick sections of my long black hair forward and curls it around my breasts. "For modesty. At first."

His hands slide beneath the thin straps of the sundress and pull them outward. With one swift movement, he tugs the dress away from my body and lets it fall to the floor.

"Mmm, perfect," he says, making sure my hair covers the front of me. "Now they're on the edge of their seat."

"Blitz..." I say, but his voice is mesmerizing.

"Now we dance, just a little." He holds my waist on one side, the other hand taking mine.

He squeezes and slides one leg toward me, his pelvis thrusting forward. I know the move. It's a rumba step, fast and long. We go forward and back.

He spins me in my panties, feet bare. The air caresses my skin, and my hair tickles the tender swollen tips of my breasts.

"It stayed in place," he says when he pulls me back in close. "We've kept it clean for the people."

His hand presses into the small of my back, just above the lace. He pulls me in very close as he continues the steps. I can feel the rough denim of his jeans against my belly. His silky shirt is a cool breath against my ribs and arms.

I reach my free hand between us and move to the buttons. "The people need to see more of their crush, their dance boyfriend," I say. "It isn't fair, keeping the lady mostly naked while you're dressed."

Our feet keep moving, forward, back, perfectly timed in the silent rumba running through both our minds.

I release the last button and push the shirt away from his chest.

His skin is warm after the cool fabric of the shirt. I want to flick my hair behind me, feel him close. But there's something erotic about the ruse. The imaginary crowd, the camera, our slow, rhythmic dance.

Blitz shrugs and the shirt slides away, landing on the edge of the bed.

I step back, then forward, then slightly to the side. I dance around him, my hands caressing his shoulders, his back, then around to his chest. We keep the rhythm, our feet moving in time.

"They're asking for more," I whisper, and catch the snap of his jeans.

"Are they?" he asks. His voice is lower now.

His zipper comes down with a soft hiss. Still we move, forward, back, just a few inches apart. I feel my hair shift and adjust to make sure I'm still covered. It's silly, but fun. I'm loving it. I push down on the jeans, and he dances right out of them as if it's a standard move you might learn in a beginner's class.

Once he's free of the pants, Blitz's footfalls slow down and become even more rhythmic. STEP, shuffle shuffle, STEP. I follow his lead, taking the hand he holds out. He turns me in to him, our bodies flush against each other, then his grip shifts, and I follow his lead, twirling out carefully, my hair heavy and in place.

His hand changes position, and he pulls me in sharply. I spin wild, my hair flying, but before I can be exposed, I'm against him, skin to skin, crushed against him.

"You think they saw?" he asks.

"Too fast," I say.

"They'll freeze frame it," he argues.

"True. The censors will shut us down."

We dance close now, allowing nothing to show, along the length of the bed and near the side table where the breakfast dishes sit from this morning.

"We've blown PG. Let's move into R," he says.

"Let's," I say.

He picks up a piece of mango from the bowl.

"What are you going to do with that?" I ask.

He slides it along my shoulder, then trails his mouth in its wake.

Our dance steps slow down, a bare whisper of feet across the floor.

"Delicious," he says, and shifts his body away. My

71

skin cools quickly without the warmth of his chest against mine.

"Now the cameras slide in," he says huskily.

The mango skims my collarbone, down the swell of my breast. The chill of it sends goose bumps rising along my skin.

But his lips are warm. His tongue slips along the path of the mango, resting on the tip of my nipple.

Then he takes me fully in his mouth, and I forget the steps, my feet faltering in our dance. His arm comes around my back for support as he leans in, taking his time with each long, carefree caress of his mouth on my body.

The sensation of falling steals my breath, then I land on the soft, airy puff of the comforter. Blitz slips the bit of mango into his mouth and licks his fingers.

The room is gauzy and half-lit, light glowing through the sheers. Blitz puts a knee on the bed near my thigh and crawls up and over me, his face near mine.

My hands slide up his knees and thighs, resting on the silky pale blue of his boxers. Because we've so recently done the show, his hair is TV perfect in its cut and layers, his eyebrows sculpted. He's perfect. The world's crush.

And mine.

His lips land on my mouth, sweet from the

mango. We grip each other, hanging on, communicating in gasps and the meeting of tongues.

Blitz slides down, his mouth trailing my body again, stopping in favorite places. The hollow of my throat. The valley between my breasts. The rise of the base of my ribs. Belly button.

He arrives at the white panties with faint yellow polka dots. "So cute," he breathes against them, moving farther down, his breath warming between my thighs.

I relax into the bed, eyes closed, feeling him, luxuriating in his attention. Blitz takes his time. His fingers lock around the lacy edge of the panties and slide them down with aching slowness.

The fabric slips along my skin, down my thighs, catching at the back of my knees. He has to shift to pull them down my ankles.

Then they're gone.

"I'm not sure where I want to go first," he says, making me let out a little laugh.

He lifts my leg, kissing the inside of my knee. His hair brushes against my tender parts, setting off a fierce longing.

His mouth leaves a cool trail as he makes his way up. My hips rise involuntarily, anxious for him to arrive. He's so good at what he does there. My breathing speeds up in anticipation.

He pauses high on my thigh, nibbling at a bit of skin.

"The censors have shut down the feed by now," he says.

I laugh. Silly Blitz. Still in the fantasy.

"Maybe," I say. "Or else everyone in the world is waiting to see if you're any good at—" I'm cut off abruptly when his mouth lands exactly where I want him to go.

I cry out, my body rising to meet him. I'm shocked out of whatever thought I just had, pleasure blasting out from where his tongue licks fire inside me.

I clutch his head with one hand, the other gripping the bedspread. He dives in more deeply, plundering every warm fold, and I move with him. I'm lost, desperate, clambering through waves of need.

His hands grasp my thighs, pushing my legs wider. I'm so open, so exposed, and he works me so well. He shifts his arm, slipping first one finger, then another inside me. A third slips along my skin, pressing lower, adding another layer of dark pleasure to the other sensations.

Our bodies move together, his head rocking with the movement of my belly and hips. The desperation is gathering, radiating into tight circles. I let out a long guttural sound, and then it all breaks free.

The rhythmic pulse of the orgasm starts tightly,

then rolls outward, taking over my whole body. My cries cascade over us, echoing on the walls.

Blitz plays it out, moving with me, teasing, stretching the moment for as long as it will go. I'm barely breathing again when he pulls away and neatly flips me over on the bed.

After a whisper of silk hits the floor, he crawls up behind me.

His desire is palpable, heat coming off his body. He lifts me to all fours, his hands running up my thighs, along my belly, and taking both breasts.

Then he spreads my legs a little wider, and I feel him hot and throbbing against me.

With a quick thrust, he's inside, and I almost fall forward. He twists my long hair into a knot around his hand and holds me in place, his other hand on my hip. He holds me steady as he rocks behind me, so fast and hard that I feel lightheaded.

He leans over my back. "I think they're asking for an encore," he whispers against my skin.

I brace my head on my hands, feeling every long, hard stroke reverberate through my entire body. The tension gathers a second time. "Yes," I say.

"That's my girl."

He slows down, takes it a little easier, making me want it hard again, pushing back against him, letting out little groans of need.

"Faster?" he asks. "Harder?"

"Yes," I tell him.

But he doesn't give it to me right away, slowing down just another touch until I'm clutching the bedding. "Please," I add.

He lets go of my hair and holds my hips with both hands. His body slams into mine, and I let out a small scream. Then again, and again, and again, until everything is obliterated in the shocking heat blasting through me with every movement.

I tighten around him, the groan low in my throat. Every muscle is pushed to the limit. This orgasm is like a big, heavy wave taking me down. I want to collapse, but Blitz holds me up, making me his, the warmth of him flowing into me.

I can barely breathe, my arms shaking, my breath stolen. Still, my insides pulse around him, greedy, gloating, willing this to go on forever.

Blitz falls over my back, his cheek on my neck. We hold on, letting our bodies reset, our hearts hammering in discordant rhythms, separated only by skin.

"You okay?" he asks, smoothing my hair away from my face.

I nod.

He shifts back and brings me with him so that we fall length-wise on the bed, our heads sinking into the pillows.

"Maybe we do need cameras," he says. I hear the shake in his voice.

I manage to flip my arm up to smack him lightly on the belly. "We already have enough cameras in our life," I say.

"True. The fantasy is better than the reality," he says.

I turn and snuggle into his chest. "Well, about the cameras anyway. Not about you."

He brings his arm around me, pulling me in more tightly.

"You got that right."

Chapter Nine

✿

Before we head to LA, I have to break the news to my mother that I'm having a fake wedding on camera. She's been so excited as Blitz and I plan our cruise. I hope she isn't crushed to hear I'm having to do vows on the show.

I decide to meet her and my brother at a park between their house and the dance studio. It's a happy place of memories for me.

I drive my little white car to their part of town. Ted rescued it for me from the besieged house and had to drive for two hours before he finally lost all the press. The crowd has thinned apparently, but there are still at least six photographers camped out on the sidewalk there.

I'll be glad for this to be over.

My old part of town is quiet, though. Nobody bothers anybody else here, and we go unnoticed in the park, although I do take the precaution of a big beach hat and sunglasses. My little brother Andy laughs when he sees it, but I just ruffle his shaggy brown hair.

"You've gotten big," I tell him.

"I'm supposed to!" he says, then takes off for the merry-go-round.

"He's growing up," Mom says. She has more gray strands threaded through her hair than I remember. She still wears her T-shirts and jeans. "You look well. A little skinny still."

"If I don't keep up with my ballet, I won't be for long!" I say.

We walk along the path of the park. Andy holds on to the metal pipe of the merry-go-round and runs as fast as he can along the worn dirt circle that surrounds it.

"You have a date for the cruise yet?" Mom asks.

"We're looking at October," I say.

"You decided if you're going to ask your dad or not?"

I don't answer. That's a tough one. I've only seen him a couple times since I left home two years ago. In one instance, he threatened to hit me when I borrowed the adoption papers from our church.

But last time, he was better. He stood on the

porch when Blitz and I came to take Mom and Andy out for Andy's birthday a couple months ago.

He didn't come with us, but he did look at me and nod, as if perhaps he was able to stand the sight of me now.

But that doesn't mean he'd be a good addition to the wedding. So many of his words echo in my ears, even now. *Worthless. The shame of the family.*

"I'd at least have to talk to him once or twice to know if he's really capable of being there," I say.

Mom nods. "You know, he did go to that recital. The one where Blitz proposed."

I thought I had seen him, but I wasn't sure.

"Did he say anything to you about it?"

"Just that he was glad you were going to live an honest life."

Right. Because getting married is the only way to be honest.

"What do you think?" I ask.

We circle back through the park so that we don't get too far from Andy.

"He still has a lot of anger in him," she says, her eyes on the trees as birds flit from one branch to another. "I think he'd be okay, but then I could also see that Benjamin might say something that sends him off."

"So he's a risk for wrecking the day," I say.

"Possibly."

I appreciate that she's honest. Now I have to be too.

"There's something else," I say.

Mom presses her hand to her chest. "Are you pregnant already?" she asks.

It's always about that with them.

"No," I say. "I am not pregnant. It's about the show. Blitz's — Benjamin's dance show."

"Oh, that." Her voice goes flat. I know neither she nor my dad approves of the rowdiness of *Dance Blitz*.

"They're requiring us to have a TV wedding. Live, I think. It's a big production."

Mom stops. "Really? Will they be on the cruise?" She touches her hair. "I can't do that. And Andy! I don't want him on TV!"

I can see the panic in her eyes, imagining the cameras on her, half-dressed girls dancing around Andy.

"No, no," I say quickly. "It's a separate thing. On TV."

"Two weddings then?" she asks. Her hands drop down.

"Yes. One for the cameras and one for us."

"That's a lot."

I stand beside her. The wind ruffles the edge of my floppy hat, and I hold on before it's lifted off my head.

"This should be the end of it," I say. "Benjamin just had a clause in his contract that if he marries a contestant, the wedding is the property of the franchise."

"That's so ridiculous." She shields her eyes from the glare as she peers across the park to spot Andy. He's found two other boys, and the three of them race around the equipment.

We walk in their direction.

"I wanted you to hear it from me. They'll be doing promos for it soon."

"Well, you know I don't watch television," she says.

"Someone might mention it," I say.

She nods.

We sit on a bench and watch the boys play.

"I guess it will be all right if I go without your father," she says. I can tell she isn't convinced, though.

"You okay mom? With Dad? He gets so angry."

"Sure. It's fine. I made a vow. For better, for worse." She still looks out over the park.

"That's not a death sentence," I say.

"Neither is being married to him," she shoots back.

I go quiet at that. Andy and the two other boys dart up the ladder to the slide and disappear in the curving plastic tube. They don't come out the end.

Mom stands up, alarmed, then sits down again when the three boys fall into a heap at the bottom, laughing.

"He's ten, Mom," I say. "Don't you think he should at least try regular school? So he can make friends?"

"Home school was good enough for you," she says sharply.

"That sounds like Dad talking," I say.

She relaxes and pats my knee. "How about I worry about my family and you concern yourself with yours. Will you have a baby with Blitz?"

"Probably someday," I say. But my stomach turns just thinking about it. I have a daughter, Gabriella. What would I one day tell another child about the missing sister?

"When you have a daughter, you will understand," she says.

I almost jump off the bench. I did have a daughter. A daughter she and my father forced me to give away.

But like her, I take deep breath and let it go.

Those things are the past.

Blitz and these two weddings are my immediate future.

83

Chapter Ten

We head down the stairs of the private plane and onto the tarmac the next day. I'm surprised to see Jessie standing by the hired car that will escort us to our hotel.

I rush up to her and envelop her in a huge hug. "Hannah found you!"

Her hair has grown long, lustrous and brown. She's still tiny, like the dancer she was before her injury led her to be my assistant on *Dance Blitz*.

She's over a year older, probably eighteen now, and seems more self assured in a classic black skirt, footless tights, and a pretty, pale blue cashmere vest. I haven't seen her since the last episode of season three, after I won the competition.

Blitz and I slide into the back seat of the car. Jessie sits up front.

"What have you been doing?" I ask her.

"I auditioned for a lot of ballets, but only got one short two-weekend thing," she says. She buckles in and picks up the same sling bag I remember her carrying before. A wave of nostalgia hits me.

"Anything we can help with?" Blitz asks.

She shrugs. "Not sure. I'm healed, but maybe I don't look as good as I think I do."

"We'll call our trainers," Blitz says. "And call Devon. Tell him I want you and Livia to do some dancing together on camera while we do the preparations for the wedding. Get you some exposure."

"That's good," I say. "Can she be a bridesmaid? That would get the cameras on her."

"Oh, you'll want to know about that," Jessie interjects.

We both look at her.

"What have they done now?" Blitz asks.

The driver starts the car, and Jessie pauses to give him the address of the hotel. Then she turns to us again.

"You're definitely not going to like it," Jessie says. "It's an obvious bid for conflict and ratings."

My stomach drops. I have a feeling I know what she's going to say.

"Are they contestants?" I ask.

Jessie nods. "The worst."

"Not Giselle," I say.

85

"Not yet," she adds quickly. "But we do have the stripper from season two."

"What!" I say. "I thought they decided she was too risky."

Blitz pulls out his phone. "They have not consulted me on any of this. I'm a producer and I'm about to pull rank."

I sit back in my seat and look out the window at the LA sights whizzing by. I can still picture the girl and the red satin bed. That sexy dance. Her crazy decision to go naked on the show to try and get Blitz's attention.

Now she's back.

All the girls who failed to impress him the first time are back. And it's worse now, because many of them have had a taste of fame and what it's like to get lost in obscurity again.

They'll want the fame back.

Blitz sits with the phone pressed to his face. "Voicemail," he says to me. "Someone's about to get an earful."

I'm not sure who he's called. Lance, maybe, although he was always in league with Giselle. Maybe Taya. This whole thing is her brainchild.

Blitz leaves a terse message to call him immediately or he's ditching the whole show and stabs another line in his contact list.

Jessie peers around her seat. "How are you?" she asks me.

"Wishing life were quiet again."

"I was surprised to hear you were doing a live wedding."

"Contracts," I say. "I guess Hannah contacted you?"

"Someone from the network," she says. "I told them I'd do it as long as it didn't conflict with any shows that might come up."

"Absolutely let us know if you get something and need to go. I can carry my own script."

She smiles. "Everything is a long shot for me. It will be fun."

Blitz shoves his phone back in his pocket again. "Either they're all in the same meeting or they're trying to shut me out." His face is stormy and dark. "I'm tempted to get right back on a plane."

Jessie sorts through a sheaf of papers. "There's a meeting this afternoon with the crew," she says. "Two o'clock. Maybe they can clear things up?"

"Doubtful," he says. "They seem to enjoy springing stuff on us."

"That's the only thing today," Jessie says. "Tomorrow will be a cake tasting," she says. "Looks like wardrobe will arrive at your hotel at eight to select your outfits. Filming is at 11."

"What else?" Blitz asks.

Jessie shifts through the pages. "Blitz meets with his trainer tomorrow afternoon. There's going to be a groomsmen dance."

"Who are the groomsmen?" he asks.

"Barry, the announcer. Mack. A couple celebrities. Looks like Dylan Wolf is going to sing. In honor of your San Antonio heritage, there will be some rodeo cowboy. Brady Wilson? He's a rather famous bull rider."

"Is Blitz going to have to kiss another pig?" I ask with a laugh.

"Funny," Blitz says. "What is the cowboy going to do?"

"It's not clear," Jessie says. "The wedding ceremony itself isn't outlined yet."

"The meeting," I say.

Blitz sits back in his seat, eyes on the roof of the car. "I can't believe we're doing this." He reaches for my hand. "Are you sure, Livia?"

I'm not, really, but I squeeze his fingers. "I think it could be fun. Let's figure out who we can help with it, like Jessie here, and make it something good."

Blitz snaps his fingers. "Let's do a fundraiser. Maybe to start more wheelchair ballerina classes in other places."

My eyes widen. "If we do that, do you think we could convince them to bring the Dreamcatcher class to the wedding?"

He smiles at that. "I like where this is going. Yes. We could."

"That would be perfect." I want Gabriella there. I wasn't sure Gwen would let her go on the cruise, but surely she would let her come to this. Those girls love Blitz beyond belief. We would pay their way. And with several of the girls here, it would hide that she is special to us.

"What about your parents?" he asks. "Your mom and brother?"

"Mom said no way to cameras," I tell him. "So there won't be family on my side. What about you?"

"I don't think Dad will go for this," Blitz says. "And he's way too offensive."

"True," I say.

Jessie looks through the pages. "Funny," she says. "They don't talk about family at all."

Blitz and I exchange glances. "I wonder why that is," he says.

Jessie frowns. "You'll have to ask them at the meeting."

We arrive at the hotel with just enough time to drop off our things and get right back in the car for the studio.

The three of us are silent on the ride. I realize we have a driver I don't know and ask Blitz, "Where's Duke?"

"No telling," he says. "He's done with Mack, as far as I know. You want him?"

"He's good for comedic relief," I say. "I wonder why he isn't a groomsman."

"He's the help," Blitz says.

"But he was your best friend," I say.

"Two years ago." Blitz shrugs. "I barely talk to him now."

We turn onto the studio lot and pause by the guard. Once we're waved through, Jessie passes the scripts back. "In case I don't get to stay."

"I wonder if my illustrious agent will be there," Blitz says.

"She'll be protecting her percentage," I say.

The driver stops the car by the back entrance to the studio and hurries around to open the door.

A couple of people are talking near the wall, but no one we know. They're taking pictures of the sky.

Not again.

I glance up.

There's no picture this time. No boobs or banana.

Just three words.

Blitz glances up and shakes his head. He takes my hand. "Ignore it," he says.

It's hard for me to drag my gaze from the white letters against the blue sky. It's like my greatest fear and worst nightmare rolled into one.

It says, "Happily ever never."

Chapter Eleven

The meeting reminds me of the one we had a long time ago, when we got dragged into the extra season where I had to go up against Giselle, Mariah, and Christy, the season two finalists.

Except that this time, there is a seat for me.

Blitz's agent Hannah is there. And the producers I know. Drake Addler, the nice one. Lance, the red-faced, not-so-nice one. Taya, who is pushy. And the other woman, whose name I've forgotten.

Bennett isn't there now, though. He sold his share to Blitz.

Devon stands in the corner, looking tired in his black turtleneck. Amara, the choreographer, sits primly nearby.

Another man clears his throat. "Blitz, Livia, good to see you. Do sit down."

After a moment, I remember who he is. Liam, the lawyer for the show. He's the one who had me sign my contract.

"Larry, you might as well cuddle up to Liam," Blitz says. Larry is his personal lawyer. "And thanks for coming."

"No prob," Larry says.

I haven't seen Larry in a long time. I give him a little wave and he smiles.

Jessie hurries through the door and sets her bag in a corner.

"Who is this?" Taya asks. She pushes back a section of her carefully blown out blond hair. She looks ready to eat somebody.

"Our assistant," Blake says. "Shelly is overseas."

"I'm here," Hannah says. "I can handle whatever goes on here."

"Jessie stays," Blitz says.

Poor Jessie isn't used to this level of scrutiny or the laser-hard glare of Hannah. "I can go," she says.

"I can make use of her," Taya says, pushing a stack of papers toward the middle of the table. "Pass these out."

Jessie glances at us to see if we agree.

I stand up. "I'll help." I'm not going to have them make Jessie feel like a second-class citizen on my watch.

Everyone is quiet while Jessie and I pass around

the packets. It looks like the treatment for the wedding episode. The cover reads, "Non-Season Special Drama."

They got the drama part right.

I sit back down next to Blitz. He takes my hand.

Taya talks first. "Our counsel Liam has the pertinent part of Blitz's contract available as we go into our first discussion of the treatment. We already have a crew on hand, and filming begins tomorrow. We didn't want the engagement to get stale before we started promoting."

I glance at Blitz. He's grimaced at the word *stale*.

"How did a prime slot open so quickly?" Lance asks. He flips through the pages.

"The hundred-year birthday celebration of that comic got canceled," Taya says. "He apparently isn't well enough."

Lance nods. "It's good timing. Sweeps week. All of it."

"Agreed," Taya says. "That's why we're jumping."

"What's the legal details?" Blitz asks. "I'm not clear on whether we're getting the marriage license and actually having official documents signed? I'm not for that. Livia and I have our own actual wedding planned."

Taya flips through the document. "If you go to page six, you'll see we have a segment planned where you apply for your marriage license. We're still working on permits for that, so it might get nixed."

"And if we do get permits," Blitz says.

Larry speaks up, casual in his tan suit with an open throat. "I checked on this. Even if you file for the permit, it can be allowed to expire. It doesn't mean anything unless you have an official sign the marriage document."

Liam is next, a more strait-laced lawyer in a black suit and red tie. "We can fake that even if it's part of the wedding filming. Use a false document and let the other one expire." He looks around at Taya and the producers. "Were you even going to do a shot of them signing? It's not wise to show the real document regardless."

Devon waves his hand to shoo away the idea. "That's boring. Nobody cares about documents."

"But city hall," Taya says. "That's an expensive segment."

"No, we'll do that one if we can," Devon says. "No close-up on documents. But I doubt we get the go ahead on our timeframe. They're notoriously difficult in LA about government offices."

"That's a big budget item we can strike," Lance says. "Might as well."

"It's good for the promo slots if we can do it, though," Devon says. "Blitz and Livia will be more relatable if we show that they are like everyone else. Make them stand in line looking nervous."

"But the cake tasting and tux fitting are much sexier promo ops," Taya says. "Nobody skips past a commercial of people doing those things."

"It's as much the social media market as the television spots," Drake says. "The media team can make a funny meme about the line at the license office."

"True," Lance says with a laugh. "Famous celebrity. Still impossible line."

Devon nods. "Exactly. We'll get a shot of some sour-faced official and it will go viral."

"Let's talk about the bridesmaids," I say, forcing my voice not to quiver. "I don't get to choose any of them?"

"We need the bridesmaids to be television worthy," Taya says. "You can save your real friends for the ceremony you and Blitz plan yourselves."

"And you left family out," Blitz says.

Now there is a discomforting silence.

"My parents won't be involved regardless," I say quickly.

"Blitz, did you talk to your brother?" Taya asks. "He's a handsome devil."

"No," Blitz says. "And my father is out."

"You want your mother?" Drake asks. "It has to be good to have his mother, right?"

"We agreed that family wasn't necessary. We want a spectacle, not a home movie," Taya says.

"We would like a social cause attached to the event," Blitz says smoothly. "I think it plays better if all this glittery celebrity has a heart."

Taya frowns. "It's a bit late to be adding a component of that nature."

Liam leans forward. "We have to get a green light from the charity before we can mention them. What did you have in mind?"

Blitz looks over at me. "We think the wheelchair ballerinas will take the fans back to the early days when Livia and I were together. It was a moment that reconnected me with them too. We want them here for the wedding. All the girls and their families. And we want to fund some classes for wheelchair dancers here in LA."

A mild uproar erupts. Everyone talks at once, as if we've just suggested bombing a third-world country.

Taya lifts her hands to shush everyone. "We appreciate your ideas," she says. "And it sounds like a worthy cause. But that's an undertaking we could never get through legal and finance in time."

"You got this show through legal and finance," Blitz counters.

Liam speaks up. "This episode was built in from the beginning," he says. "With legal and finance. What you're proposing is basically starting a new organization. The federal non-profit paperwork alone would take months."

"Aren't there any wheelchair dance programs here already?" I ask.

"Possibly," Liam says. "But many of them wouldn't have the infrastructure or personnel to handle an influx of money of this size. Plus manage the publicity we'd suddenly give them."

"And I don't think there's a budget item for flying in a bunch of random people," Taya says, her tone dismissive. "Plus, contracts. And liability for travel for these girls."

The room goes quiet.

I'm the one who speaks up next. "Is there anything about this wedding that belongs to me and Blitz?" I ask quietly.

"It's still you," Drake says. "And Blitz." He passes his hand over his forehead, like this is all too much. "This one is for the fans. They just want to see the couple they feel they brought together in pretty clothes they will never own, eating fancy food they will never taste. And having the fantasy wedding they could only dream up. They put you here, in their minds. So, this is their wedding too."

I glance over at Blitz. I can see he's softening on the matter. The wheelchair ballerinas were a long shot. And I can see it might be hard to get them to travel. Daisy for sure, who often has bad days. Flying is hard.

Maybe a local wedding is better than a cruise. Make it easy for the girls to come.

My mind is a whirl as the meeting goes on, budgets and schedules and filming days. We will be doing so little at the studio itself that they decide not even to open it to save the crew costs.

I only register that the meeting is over when chairs start scraping the floor and everyone begins to stand.

I get up, a little dazed.

"So we're all set for wardrobe tomorrow and filming at the cake shop?" Taya asks.

"All set," Devon says. "I'll get the footage over and the first promo is set for a week from now."

"You can get it ready in time?" Lance asks.

"Not a problem," Devon assures him.

Hands shake all around.

Blitz and I walk out with Larry and Jessie.

"I'm surprised you didn't fight them on the bridesmaids," Larry says. "Livia's contract doesn't specify that she loses the right to choose them."

I shrug. "I don't think Mindy's parents would let her come, and everyone at the dance studio is so busy. We couldn't have Danika shut it down while we film."

Larry nods. "All right then. Good luck with that

part." He shakes Blitz's hand. "Let me know if anything goes south."

"I'm sure it will," Blitz says.

"And if you want that charity set up in the future, just let us know. We can handle the paperwork."

"Thanks," Blitz says.

We walk ahead of the rest of the group, not really wanting to engage in random chit-chat. The sun is bright overhead. Perpetual summer in sunny southern California.

But I can't help but feel like there's a permanent cloud over my head.

Chapter Twelve

The cake shop is a cute little place in a restored Victorian house. I feel like I've seen it before, so maybe allowing film crews is a side business. That's pretty common in LA.

I wear a white sundress with a blue belt. It's light and pretty. They've dressed Blitz very classically in fitted khaki pants and a pale blue shirt. No leather and sexy. He's a family man now, apparently.

A ridiculously long white limo takes us to the shop. We have to be filmed exiting it about six times before Devon lets us move on.

Inside, Amara speaks to a woman in a white apron. This other lady has a makeup person hovering around her like a bee, so I assume she's the one who will be filming with us.

"Why is Amara here?" I ask Blitz. "Are we dancing?"

"It wasn't in the script," he says.

The woman looks up and shoos the makeup girl away. "You're here!"

"Just an hour behind schedule," Devon says. "That's good for us."

We do introductions. The woman is Marcy, and she owns the shop. Everything inside is picture perfect. Blitz pokes at a fully decorated cake sitting on a shelf nearby. "Fake," he whispers to me and I giggle.

"We're going to do five or six entrances and greetings," Devon says, looking around. "Lighting has things well in hand."

A half-dozen rigs are erected in various spots around the room.

"We'll have them sit here," Marcy says, gesturing to two fancy wire stools with heart-shaped backs. "Or we can do a low table over there." She points to a marble-topped desk with three chairs.

"I like the bar," Devon says. "We'll see how it looks."

The camera man sets up inside the door. "Ready for test shots."

A young man sets down a coil of thick cords and elbows Jessie. She sets down her messenger bag, and the two of them go outside the door.

"And in three, two, one," the camera operator says.

The two of them come in, and Devon steps behind the camera. As they reposition lights and move a couple items from shelves, Blitz and I wander the little shop.

Amara approaches. "So, after Devon scouted the place, he thought maybe you two could dance a little over there." She gestures to an open area in front of the glass cake display, where customers would normally wait in line.

"What sort of dance?" Blitz asks.

"Nothing fancy. A waltz. Something that doesn't take too much space."

"Sure," Blitz says. "Will we have music, or will it be added in post?"

"Both," Amara says. "The idea is that you will start on your own, then the music will be slowly added. Sort of a cinema effect. We'll play the piece, so you can get the tempo and steps roughly in time."

Blitz takes my hand and leads me to the space. "Something like this?"

He draws me close, and we begin a slow dance, one-two-three, one-two-three.

"Sure," she says. "Let's not do classic head position, though. More like if you were at your wedding. So you can see each other."

We pull apart slightly to give us room for noses as

we look into each other's eyes. My skirt flutters around as we move, Blitz careful to keep us from crashing into chairs or counters. The crew moves aside to give us space.

"Okay," Devon says. "We're good for the entrance. Places."

Blitz and I break apart. Kendra pops up from a chair to fix my hair and give me another light dusting of powder. "No more dancing until it's time to film," she says. "It's warm in here and you shine."

"In a good way," Blitz says, kissing my nose.

Kendra pushes him away with a half-annoyed snort. "Don't be messing with the powder." She brushes me again. "And no kissing or eating unless you're told!"

"Aye, aye, captain!" Blitz says with a laugh.

We step back outside, and a crew member closes the door.

"She's not watching," Blitz says, leaning down to press a light kiss on my mouth.

"You're terrible," I say.

Behind us, an assistant speaks into her headset. "How far back?" she asks.

She motions us back a few more steps. "All right."

Blitz and I wait for her instructions.

"Okay," she says. "Hold hands and walk side by side. Blitz, open the door with your right hand. The door pushes in. Marcy will be just inside. On my command. Wait. And, go! Smile!"

Blitz and I walk forward. He opens the door. Marcy is in place.

"Blitz! Livia!" She walks forward and extends a hand.

"Cut!" Devon says. "Did we agree on a shake or a hug?"

"Livia's dress is white," Kendra says. "A hug might get makeup on either one of them."

"Marcy, shake with both hands around one of theirs," Devon says. "Make it warmer than a business shake."

The crew opens the door and we go back outside again.

It takes twelve tries before Devon is happy. Finally, we take a seat at the counter.

"We have six types of cake for you to try," Marcy says. Each tiny round cake is decorated with a different color flower on top. She points to the first one.

"Cut," Devon says. "Blitz and Livia, back away a second so we can get a clear shot of the cakes. B roll!"

"I'm surprised they didn't shoot that ahead," Blitz says.

Kendra hurries forward to adjust my lipstick. "They were supposed to, but the original cakes didn't look good enough," she says. "Devon was super pissed. They had to go buy some from another bakery."

"Oh, I bet Marcy loves that," Blitz says.

We watch as Marcy repeatedly describes each small cake for the cameras. She's not a true actress, and I can see the unhappiness in her eyes that these are someone else's work. "Of course, your cake won't be decorated like these samples in any way."

That must be her little stab at whoever's cakes these are.

"Okay, back to the counter!" Devon says.

Marcy cuts sections of cake from each flavor. We film various silly bits where Blitz and I feed each other. One of the cakes is some sort of herbal poppy-seed wheat, and Blitz can't hide his disgust.

Marcy barely holds it together for that one. She can probably already see the entertainment news going bonkers over footage of Blitz hating on a cake that isn't even from her shop.

That's show business.

After what seems like hours of cake footage, Marcy takes our "order." Once that is done, it's our moment to dance.

"Just keep rolling," Devon says.

Blitz takes my hand and helps me off the stool. We wander the shop as if entranced by her designs, a small favor to her that will hopefully get used and make up for the switched-out cakes.

"I can't believe our day is finally coming," Blitz says and takes my hand to turn me in a circle.

He draws me close. This is classic Blitz, dazzling and full of charm.

"Me either," I say.

We begin a slow, lazy dance. Music fills the shop, and I must admit, I'm caught up in it. The lovely room. The smell of sugar and warm cake.

The floor creaks as we cross the wooden boards. They'll definitely have to drop in their own music to get rid of that.

The door opens and closes. Odd they'd let the crew go in or out while they're filming. That's not just sound to filter out, but a flash of light that crossed us from the sun.

"Oh, isn't this just charming," I hear.

Oh my God. No way.

No.

Blitz lets my hand go, and I whip around to see her.

Giselle.

"What are you doing here?" I ask, about to look for Devon, when my face is suddenly wet and cold.

I touch my cheeks. They're covered in red.

What is this? I panic for a moment, thinking it's blood, and wipe it off as fast as I can. Slowly, I realize it's something else, sweet smelling and sticky. I look up, red dripping onto my dress, and lock on Giselle.

She holds a can of spray frosting, the nozzle still aimed at me.

"Put THAT on your wedding cake," she says.

"What the hell!" Blitz says. He pulls me in close, hands wiping at the frosting on my face. "Who the hell put her up to this?"

We look around, but nobody seems surprised but us. And Jessie. Her mouth is wide open in a shocked "o."

"Get out of here," Blitz roars at Giselle. "And shut off that damn camera."

The main camera operator looks over a Devon. He signals to keep rolling. I glance over at the second camera man. He's smiling, like he's loving every minute of his job.

I look down at my pretty white dress. It's ruined, deep red stains from the frosting all down the front. I don't have any way to clean my hands or face.

"This is the last straw," Blitz says to the room. "Don't think I'm going to continue the contract if this is the type of bullshit you're going to pull."

Giselle laughs. "You should see yourself, Blitz," she says. "So serious now. Have a little fun, like we used to." She squirts a little more frosting in the air.

"Nothing about this is fun," Blitz says. He lunges forward and snatches the frosting bottle from her. "And I hope they're paying you well, because this is the end of the line for you. You are easily the most hated woman in America."

She shrugs. "There's a career in villainy."

"Not if nobody wants to work with you because you pull stunts like this," Blitz fires back.

The shop owner holds a pink dish towel in her hands, but she looks afraid to pass it to me. Nobody seems to want to move.

Blitz spots her and storms over to grab the towel. "Shut the cameras off or I will sue this entire operation into oblivion and not a single frame will see the light of day."

He walks up and wipes at my cheeks. "I am so sorry, Livia. I had no idea."

The trance on everyone else seems to be broken as there's a sudden flurry of activity.

Jessie runs up. "I'll get more towels," she says. We've already covered this one in frosting.

The secondary camera man tries to approach with his rig, but Blitz turns with a threatening stance. "You take one more second of footage and I will smash that thing."

The man puts the camera down.

Kendra shakes her head as she comes up to me. "Sometimes I hate this business. There's a bathroom back here. Let's go."

Giselle has stepped aside, leaning against the wall, a smirk on her face.

"I want her OUT of here," Blitz says. "Or this whole deal is off!"

"I thought you said it was already off," Giselle says with a laugh. "Blitz, you really have to think before you talk."

I don't hear any more because we enter the bathroom and close the door.

I have no idea what will happen from here.

Chapter Thirteen

✻

Blitz calls an emergency meeting that night. Only Drake Addler is actually in town, so we have to do it by video conference.

My face is still a little pink in places from the frosting stain. Kendra is supposed to come by later with some sort of cleanser that will take it off. Regular soap isn't cutting it, no matter how much I scrub.

I stay out of range of the web cam as Blitz conducts the meeting. There is plenty of shouting on his end. Drake and Taya assure him that the order to bring in Giselle didn't come from them.

"We have given Devon free reign," Taya says.

"We need to discuss his future in this production," Blitz says. "What happened was uncalled for. If he wants to save this show on the back of Livia's humiliation, I will kill the franchise myself."

"I'll speak to Devon," Taya says. "I'll make it understood that this is supposed to be a sweet, lovely fantasy. Giselle is disrupting it."

Blitz motions me over. I hesitate but walk a little closer. "I want you to say it to her. She's the one Giselle is going after."

The screen is split to show all their faces. I give a little wave.

"We're so sorry," Drake says. "Devon was out of line."

I want to say that everyone had to be in on it, not just Devon, but I don't. It doesn't matter now. It's done.

Blitz shuts down the computer. "I don't buy it," he says. "Nobody was surprised."

"Jessie was," I say.

"Is that the only person loyal to us?" he asks. "Jessie?"

"I guess they're worried about their next paycheck. What's the word on the next season?"

Blitz pushes away from the desk and heads to the sofa. He looks tired. I know how he feels. I'm tired too. And pink.

"They're not casting the next bachelor until after our wedding. The network isn't positive the show can sustain another season."

He plunks down, letting his head fall back on the black leather. I sit beside him and lay my head on his shoulder. His T-shirt is soft and warm. He puts his arm around me.

"You think they'll try something else to boost ratings?" I ask.

"I don't know," Blitz says. "Is Devon working alone? Is someone paying Giselle?"

"Lance was noticeably absent from the call."

"I know," Blitz says. "He's always had a thing for Giselle."

"Why is she doing this? Can't she move on?"

"Not until she's got somewhere to go. This is her best shot at staying on people's minds."

We sit for a while, just close and quiet. Eventually Kendra buzzes us from the lobby and we send her up.

Blitz stays on the sofa as Kendra and I head to the bathroom. The pink is definitely faded, but in the harsh lights over the mirror, I can still see an outline of a reddish tint along one cheek.

"Stupid cheap dye in that stuff," Kendra says, turning over a bottle and soaking a cotton ball.

"When did you find out it was going to happen?" I ask her.

She stares at the yellow-soaked cotton for a moment.

I don't know if she'll be truthful. I've never been close with Kendra. I only see her on shooting days when she comes to do the styling of our clothes and the set. But she has been with *Dance Blitz* since the first season. Surely she cares at least a little about the show's reputation. And Blitz.

She sighs and lifts her hand to rub the cotton ball on my cheek. "This morning. Just before you got there, we got the briefing about a surprise visitor. Nobody knew about the frosting. I assure you that."

"Who told you?"

"Devon," she says. "I think the plan was for Giselle to show up and provoke Blitz to say some things that would make for good promo clips. I'm pretty sure the frosting was her idea."

This makes sense. Giselle would see an opening and take it to the next level.

I'll have to tell Blitz this. He might not be as angry with Devon if he knows it was just the usual antics that were planned.

"She's supposed to be a bridesmaid, you know," Kendra says. "I got the specs on her dress and all. Maybe they're keeping it hush hush, but I know her measurements."

My stomach turns to lead. Giselle, at the wedding? If she's willing to do frosting on camera, what will she do during the ceremony?

"Surely they won't let her after this," I say.

"You never can tell. Dance Blitz has been a cash cow." She drops the cotton ball and turns my cheek to the light. "It's not just the show. But all the merchandizing and reruns and DVD. It's a lot to lose."

She soaks another ball and runs it over my skin. "We've just about got this."

The lights buzz as she works. Otherwise the suite is silent.

Finally, Kendra sits back. "I think we've got it."

"Thank you for helping. I would have no idea how to get that color off."

She nods and tosses the used cotton into the trash. "I'll keep my ear to the ground about what's planned for tomorrow's bridesmaid outing. I'll let Jessie know if anything is untoward."

"I guess she was supposed to be a surprise again?" I ask.

"I can only assume. There is definitely a dress in her size waiting to be tried on at the salon tomorrow."

Suddenly I'm dreading this thing. I already have to face red-silk naked girl. And now Giselle? There isn't a single one of the ten bridesmaids on the list that I know. Mariah and Christy, the other two finalists from my season, turned it down. I don't blame them, really.

And if Giselle would spray frosting, what would the red-silk girl do? Have a wardrobe malfunction during the vows?

Kendra packs away her bottles and cotton. "I can see this whole thing is a strain on you. You can always walk away."

"Sixty-three million dollars," I say.

She nods. "I get it. But sometimes you have to wonder what the price of your freedom is."

I walk her to the door. Blitz just waves from the sofa, his face covered with his arm.

When she's gone, I stand with my back to the wall, looking at him, casual in sweats and a T-shirt, his foot tapping with anxiety. He looks anxious, miserable.

We both are.

How much should we have to sacrifice to *Dance Blitz*?

Chapter Fourteen

Wardrobe arrives at six in the morning since our filming is at nine. The bridal shop we're invading has only given Devon until noon, and then they have to be open for normal business.

Kendra isn't here, but my favorite hairdresser Cecilia is. She gives me a long hug. "I hear things went south yesterday," she says.

"Please tell me you didn't know about Giselle," I say.

"Not a bit. We're all pissed as hell. If you quit, game's over for us," she says.

"Don't you work other shows?" I ask.

"Sure, but nobody has a budget like this!" she says. "It takes four other gigs to make up for this one. That's why we're all still here."

She sits me down at the bathroom mirror. "Let's

give you your crown. Today we're taking you from princess to *queen*."

She works on my hair while the others fiddle with the dress and argue about shoes. A makeup artist arrives to give me a *clean, pure look*, so she says. I wonder what sort of look they're giving red-silk girl. And somebody is probably working on Giselle.

They're efficient and quick, so by seven-thirty, we're packing to leave. Blitz is still in his sweats. He has the day off. The early wedding planning is mostly about me, although he does have a tux shoot tomorrow.

Maybe that's where they'll send red-silk girl. My stomach knots.

Blitz comes to the door as we head out. "I'd tell you to break a leg, princess, but maybe break one of theirs," he says. He's a lot calmer about this now that he knows Devon didn't plan the frosting part of the stunt.

I laugh and kiss his head. "Or two."

"That's my girl," he says.

The entire entourage walks the hall and piles into the elevator. When we get to the bottom, there's a security detail of three bodyguards, including long lost Duke. We move together in a group, me and Duke at the center.

"You're back!" I say. "Mack not need you?"

"Mack is all done until his DVD release," he says. "I'm back with you and Blitz for the moment."

He walks alongside us in his cowboy hat and sunglasses. His blue jeans and red plaid shirt make him stand out from the other security in all black. The lobby is mostly empty, but he keeps his eye out as we move to the front door.

"Why aren't we using the private exit?" I ask.

"Filming starts outside," he says.

I stop in my tracks. "What?"

The wardrobe and makeup people disperse, including Cecilia. I feel naked and exposed, even with Duke and three other men surrounding me.

The glass doors to the outside slide open and Jessie bursts through. She runs in, spots us, and rushes toward me.

"Okay, heads up," she says. "Full film cameras out there. About four or five hundred fans. All the brides-maids inside the car," she says.

The wardrobe people clump together near a cluster of sofas to watch.

"Giselle?" I ask.

"No," she says.

"How many girls?"

"Nine," Jessie says.

"So missing one," I say.

"She was supposed to be there?" Jessie asks.

"We suspect."

Duke shakes his head. "Gonna be a fun morning!" He presses his finger to his ear, and I see he has a tiny earbud there. "We gotta move." He takes my arm and tries to lead me forward.

I plant my feet and refuse to go. "Anything else?" I ask Jessie.

"There's a camera in the limo," Jessie says. "I'm guessing they want to see your reaction to the other girls."

"We really have to go," Duke says.

"Shut it," I say. "You're sure Giselle wasn't in there?"

"Totally sure," Jessie says.

"Okay." I stand a little straighter. "Let's go."

Duke leads us to the doors.

"You have to go over there," Duke says to Jessie, pointing to where the rest of the crew has stepped aside. "Only Livia and bodyguards go out those doors right now."

He seems perturbed at her. I know she can't be in the shot, but I don't understand why he cares if she fills me in.

My hands check my hair and flutter across my cheek where the frosting stains were. When will we ever be free of this madness?

When we approach the doors, Duke and the other security guards step away from me so that I appear to be alone as I exit.

As soon as I step through, the crowd goes crazy.

I take it all in. Devon and the main camera are to the right. A second camera on a ladder is to the left. The sleek black limo is directly in front with a fancy doorman I've never seen. He wears an outlandish old-fashioned red uniform like some bygone era. He nods at me.

A barrier made of white sawhorses separates the crowd from the circle. Gosh, they're having to redirect all the regular people coming to the hotel somewhere else for me. Another reason to leave so early in the morning.

I wave at the fans and the noise intensifies. I remember to smile. They are the best part. Although they feed the insanity. When things get crazy, they tune in. When we're living normal lives, they move elsewhere.

And that's what makes everyone on the show panic. That there will be no interest from the fans.

Who can live this way for long? Desperately seeking attention? Fearing your career is dead if you don't feed it?

A sea of faces flash by. Singers. Actors. Rock stars. How do they face this, day in and day out?

"This way, Livia," the doorman says, pulling on the handle to the limo.

I have to trust that this part will go fine.

I wave once more to all the bystanders and step forward.

Then I hear someone call out.

"Livia! Oh, Livia!"

I look up.

Seriously?

It's Giselle, all prettied up in a pink dress, her hair a perfect blond updo. "I'm late, but I'm here!" she says.

She walks up and kisses my cheek. "I wouldn't miss this for the world!"

My head swivels hard. Who planned this?

Devon's eyebrows are up and his expression is dark. He's not happy. He got called on the carpet about yesterday, and this was not planned.

The camera guy in front of me swings his rig around, following Giselle as she heads into the limo. The other one stays on me.

Everyone waits for my response.

The security men are stoic, standing with hands clasped by their bellies.

Then I see Duke. He's come outside with the other guards. His eyes are on the form of Giselle, her pink bottom sticking out as she ducks down and pauses in the car door, looking for a place to sit inside or maybe taking a verbal assault from someone in there who knows she isn't welcome.

Duke's face turns to me, and even with the sunglasses, I see it. The self-satisfied smirk.

And the truth arrives in a flash.

It was him.

It was him all along.

Chapter Fifteen

❦

I grab his arm and catch him off balance.

"You asshole!" I hiss, knowing the crowd noise will cover it. "He trusted you!"

Duke cocks his head. He realizes what I know but plays it off. "Don't worry your pretty little self about it," he says. "Now go on and get inside the limo."

"No," I say, backing away. "I'm done. Totally and completely done."

"It's all a little fun," Duke says. "Keeps everyone in show business."

"No," I say. "This isn't fun at all."

I turn and rush back inside the hotel. The stupid heels keep me from running as fast as I like, so I kick them off and leave them in the lobby. I see why Cinderella ditched hers. I don't care who finds them.

I glance back. Devon and Duke have started to

follow, so I head for the private hall. I'm betting neither of them have a secure pass. As soon as I'm through, I slam the door shut and run to the special elevator that goes direct to the top floor of private suites.

As I expected, the others are stopped by the locked door.

I mash the button, and mercifully, the elevator is already down.

My nerves jangle so badly on the way up that I hear ringing in my ears. I try to put it all together. Duke and Giselle. It had always been Duke and Giselle. He kept getting her ways in. Fed her information. And for what? Sex? Did he care for her?

Why did betrayal always happen at the hands of a love affair?

I'm not sure the others won't convince the hotel to let them up, so as soon as my doors open, I sprint madly to the suite. The regular elevators ding down the hall, whether with *Dance Blitz* crew or others staying on this floor, I don't know. I'm not going to stand around to see.

I swipe the card key and throw myself into the room.

Blitz is standing by the mini bar, pouring orange juice.

"Livia!" he says. "What happened?"

I run to him and bury my face against his soft T-shirt. "Giselle was down there," I choke out.

"What?" His arms around me tighten. "Is she a bridesmaid?"

"I don't know." I pull away enough to look up at him. "It was Duke all along," I say. "I think they're having some sort of relationship."

"Duke?" His voice is incredulous, but I see him thinking about it. Weighing conversations, turning over bits of evidence.

He leads me over to the sofa. "Tell me exactly how it went down."

I relate to him about the crowd, Giselle's entrance, Duke's expression.

"He all but admitted it. Said it keeps everyone in show business."

Blitz rubs his eyes. "We've been best friends forever," he says.

"Did you feel something change? At any point?" I say my next words carefully. "Like maybe right before that tweet?"

Blitz leans against the back of the sofa. "Hell. I don't know. He was excited to move out here. Quit his job in construction. Loved driving my car around. Had his own place. The show paid him pretty well, let him in on stuff like the placement of the cameras. I knew there was an agreement about secret footage. He generally let me in on that stuff, gave me a heads up. We were having a good time all through season one."

"Then Giselle came on season two," I say.

"I saw a lot of her. The whole world knows that. She was great for the show. Got a lot of attention. She's probably half the reason it did so well."

"I guess she knows that."

"Probably. But something turned. She was always catty with the other contestants. That was part of her appeal. But then she got that way with me."

"Did you know why?"

"I figured it was the show. It's a tough thing for the women, feeling like you're fighting for the same guy." He glances over at me. "They think they're in love with me, but really, they're just in love with the idea of it all. Having people follow your every move. Being that 'in' couple on the cover of the tabloids."

"I never loved it."

Blitz draws me in a little closer. "You always liked me for me."

"Still do."

"I guess maybe the real reason she turned could have been Duke."

"Maybe the tweet was a way to get you out of the picture?" I suggest.

"I was super wasted that night. And I was sick of Giselle by then. They didn't have to get me to ditch her. I was already there."

"You said you never knew how it got on your social media. You just sent it to Duke."

"Yeah, but I have a whole Twitter team. When the tweet came out, we couldn't own up to that. It's an illusion that I pay that much attention to fans, retweeting and responding and all that."

I sit up straight. "So, anybody could have tweeted it? Anyone in marketing?"

"They could have, but it was like three in the morning. And it had to come from my phone. We checked that straight away. Like I said, I did write the thing. I just thought I sent it to Duke."

"Does Duke have access to your account?"

"I doubt it."

"Could he have used your phone?"

"Not unless he was here."

"Was he around?"

"He had left. That's why I sent him the message."

"Go through the events exactly."

Blitz runs his hands through his hair. "I'm out with Giselle. Duke is driving. We get to my condo, and she gets a little wild..." he trails off.

"It's fine, whatever," I say.

"Duke asks if we're done driving for the night. I say yes."

"Does he leave?" I ask.

"I assume so."

"How did he seem?"

DEANNA ROY

Blitz heads to the sofa and sinks down on it. "Pissed, I guess. Something was off. We were all off."

"And what happened next?"

"After...after Giselle is done, she crashes out. I take that picture of her and send it to Duke along with the thing about the gorilla. I was looking for someone to commiserate with."

"What did you do with your phone after that?"

"Beats me. Set it down. Probably on the charger by the bed."

"Did you stay with it?"

"I slept on the sofa, not with her. I know that much."

"Could Giselle have done it?"

His face falls. "Maybe. Why would she release what I said about her?"

"Why would she spray me with frosting?"

We both jump when someone pounds on the door.

"Livia, we have a twenty-thousand-dollar shoot that isn't happening right now."

It's Devon.

"They always think in terms of money, don't they?" I ask.

"It's their job," Blitz says. "Do I let them in?"

"I don't know," I say. "I don't want to be dragged into it again, really."

"So, let's don't," Blitz says.

"Don't what?" I ask.

"Get dragged in. Screw them. Screw the sixty-three million. Screw it all."

"Blitz! They will sue you!"

"Let them. I can't carry this show forever. Let it die. It was a terrible concept anyway."

"You ready to be poor?" I ask.

"I grew up like a normal kid," Blitz says. "I can live like a normal adult."

The banging grows louder. "Livia! We're going to have the manager let us in!" Devon calls.

"Too bad we're on the top floor," I say. "We can't escape out the window."

"We don't need to escape the room," Blitz says.

"Why not?"

Blitz picks up his phone and scrolls through his contacts. He finds "Larry the lawyer" and hits "call."

"Because it doesn't matter whether they come in or not. By the time they get here, I'll have broken the contract."

I squeeze his arm. I get it now. "And we'll have already escaped."

Chapter Sixteen

W e cancel the wedding cruise.

We don't have that kind of money right now.

The other producers have sued Blitz for breaking his contract. His assets are currently frozen.

We have to live on what I made on the show.

It's sort of fun to be the primary breadwinner.

In the outrageous aftermath of Blitz refusing to do the wedding, Duke and Giselle are spotted together. Duke all but admits they sent out the tweet about her to expose what a jerk Blitz is.

"I couldn't have him ruining my sweet Giselle's life," Duke says.

Of course, they sell their story to the tabloids and are working out a book deal.

Meanwhile, Blitz and I try to plan how to live

under the shadow of a lawsuit that will drag out for years.

I've signed up for another traveling ballet company. Blitz is negotiating DVD rights again. The last DVD did pretty well, and he thinks he can get more money for this one.

Enough to live on.

We still have our talents. Our famous names. We will get by.

One TV show can't crush us.

As for the wedding, our new plan has turned out even better than the original. Why have a fancy TV show special, or even an exclusive private cruise, when you can have everyone you love?

With a new ballet starting in a few weeks, we decide to go with a quick, easy-to-plan wedding before I go on tour.

And it's perfect.

I wait in the Dance of the Shades studio at Dreamcatcher Academy. My mother has just fastened the dozens of buttons going up the back of my gown.

It's not a designer. Not one-of-a-kind. But it was made just for me. By her.

Sheets cover the windows looking into the room from the hallway, so no one can peek before they're supposed to. Blitz mainly. He's been wandering the halls from what I hear, trying to make his way in. Crazy boy.

Mindy dashes in, her pink dress flirting with her calves. She looks prim and sweet, her dark hair pinned up, bits of baby's breath wound through it.

"The photographer is coming in a second," she says. "She says not to finish buttoning it until she's here."

Mom puts her hands on her hips. "I just finished it!"

"She'll probably just pose you like you're doing it," I say. "Don't worry." I want to tell her, this is the right level of drama. Buttons done too early.

My level of drama.

Mom arranges my curls around my shoulders. "It's not quite right," she says. "I'm afraid I'm hopeless with hair."

"Ooh!" Mindy says. "I'll be right back!" She hurries out again.

Mom shakes her head. "She's completely aflutter over that cowboy."

"Have her parents met him yet?" I ask.

"Sure. They spotted them together at the horse lessons, oh, about three months ago."

"She kept it hidden all this time?"

"Apparently."

"Did they flip?"

Mom sticks a bobby pin in her mouth, moving another section of my hair off my face. "Totally."

"I'm glad you're talking to them again," I say.

"It's good to be able to get the boys together."

Mindy returns. "I have a solution!" she says.

She turns and waves somebody inside.

It's Cecilia! Her spiky hair is tipped in yellow now.

"What are you doing here!" I gasp.

"Saving your everlovin' hair," she says. "Jessie said you had plenty of seats open and we ought to fly down if we could."

"We? Who else is here?"

"Just a few of us. Kendra. Shelly. Barry Winston came."

"Barry's here? Without cameras?"

"He's talking to the JP. I think he wants to host." Cecilia laughs. "Mama, you take a load off. You are mother of the bride, and we'll pamper your princess."

Mom hands the brush to Cecilia. "You're from the show, I take it?"

"She did my hair for all the episodes," I say.

Mindy looks like she could burst with happiness that she helped.

The photographer rushes in. "Oh, thank goodness. You're still getting ready." She starts firing shots right away.

"What's got you in a tizzy?" Cecilia asks.

She lowers the camera. "Blitz had some rather unusual ideas for the groomsmen."

"Who'd he get?" Cecilia asks, quickly working

over my hair. "Please say Chris Hemsworth. Or the Rock. Lord, have mercy if he got the Rock."

I laugh. "Nobody like that. We're reality show has-beens now."

"Hardly," the photographer says. "I already had six offers for any shots I was willing to sell. Everybody wants to see the wedding that never was."

Cecilia shakes her head. "That 'never was' is obviously happening now. I never will understand why those entertainment shows want to put a nasty spin on everything."

The door opens again, and the Dreamcatcher staff, Suze, Janel, Betsy and Aurora, walk in.

"Don't let him see!" Suze shouts with a laugh.

They slam the door with an eruption of giggles.

"Blitz?" I ask.

"That boy is desperate to get a peek at you," Suze says.

"He's gonna have to wait like everybody else," Cecilia says.

I can feel my hair sliding into place. Cecilia is working her magic.

"You look amazing," Aurora says. "We're running a little late, though."

The door opens again.

"Don't let Blitz in!" Suze cries out.

But it's Gwen.

"He's gone," she says. Her face is more serious

than the others. She catches sight of me and gives a little nod. "Thought you'd want your flower girls."

"Yes!" I say.

The bridesmaids monitor the door to make sure Blitz isn't too close by.

My eyes tear up as they roll in. Daisy. Marissa. And of course, Gabriella.

The spokes of their wheelchairs are interlaced with ribbon. Their pink dresses spill over their arm rests.

"That one is the spitting image of you," Cecilia says, gesturing to Gabriella.

I freeze, but Cecilia points to Gwen, not me. "Same hairstyle. Looks good on you both."

Mom and I catch glances and smile. Gwen touches her hair. She has a headband braid, same as Gabriella. "Gabby insisted," she says.

"Cute," Cecilia says. "Okay, we're done. Ready for this wedding march?"

Flashes go off as the photographer takes shots of me with the dance teachers and Mindy, me and the ballerinas, and me with Mom. Cecilia heads back to her seat.

Finally, Gwen leads the girls out to head to the recital hall. Mindy and the other bridesmaids follow.

It's just me and Mom.

"Did you change your mind about your father giving you away?" Mom asks.

"Is he even here?" I ask.

"He's sitting with your brother."

I shake my head. "I don't think so."

Dad still only rarely speaks to me, although he no longer gives my mother any grief for coming to visit me. He didn't come to the rehearsal dinner or any of the other events leading up to the wedding.

"I understand," she says. "Let's catch up with the others."

We head into the hall. The florist is still handing the bouquets to all the girls as they enter the main lobby.

"Everyone inside?" Mom asks as we approach.

Suze nods. "Everybody is seated."

We cross the lobby. It's beautifully decked with flowers and an ice sculpture of Blitz and I dancing, all a gift from Danika, the owner of the academy.

Off to one side, a table with the wedding cake waits, surrounded by rented crystal plates and glasses.

An ordinary reception for two regular people.

Our bodyguard Ted sees us and opens the back door to the recital hall.

Andy rushes up the aisle and out the door to us. "Livia! It's so boring in there!"

I laugh. "Weddings are a little bit dull."

"We've been waiting forever!" He tugs at the collar of his shirt, trying to loosen the little tie.

"Walk me to my seat, young man," Mom says. "And we can get this started."

"Finally!" Andy says. "I'm ready for cake!" He tries to crane his head around to get another look at it in the lobby.

"Come along," Mom says.

The two of them head up the aisle to sit in the front row. I catch a glimpse of the back of my father's head. So, he is here.

I'm not going to change my mind. He never earned the right to give me away.

"Ready?" Ted asks Marissa, who has lined up first in the procession of wheelchair ballerinas.

"Ready!" she says.

He holds the doors for her. She rolls forward, then Daisy, and then Gabriella. Gwen follows and situates them near the stage, then finds her own seat.

The bridesmaids start their walk. Janel, who teaches the wheelchair ballerinas with me. Betsy, my own ballet teacher. Suze, who works the front desk. Aurora, who teaches the toddlers. And finally Mindy, my own best friend.

No models. No professionals. No contestants. Just real people.

The photographer snaps shots of each woman. I imagine what my other wedding might have been. Video rigs and directors, makeup artists, and stylists.

All wrong.

This is all I ever wanted.

Finally, it's just me in the back. Ted holds the door.

"You look great," he says. "You're really walking on your own?"

I nod and step into the doorway. I don't have a train, so there is nothing to arrange. Just a lovely long dress with a million buttons, satin and a slim fit. And a hairdo fit for a queen. I touch it, the crown of braids at the top, the fall of curls at the bottom. It's a lot like how it looked that first time I saw Blitz Craven right here at the dance academy.

Up on the platform, Blitz comes out in his black tuxedo. Everyone murmurs as he stands there, looking out, and catches sight of me. His smile is pure Blitz, that charismatic, perfect combination of sexy and charm.

Then his brother Dante steps out, and the murmurs grow a little louder. Dante is the spitting image of his brother, but with a rogue-like, devilish quality.

Yeah, he's got a face for television. I glance at the bridesmaids to see their reaction. I think Suze is going to melt.

Beside Dante is Blitz's dad. Then Jacob, our friend here at Dreamcatcher. He was one of the first people who ever knew about us. He kept the secret.

"I guess I should get up there," Ted says. "You all right?"

I nod. "Go on."

Ted dashes behind the back row and comes up the side. He waves to Andy, who leaves my mom and heads up the steps to finish out the groomsmen.

The music grows louder, a four-piece stringed group playing from the far right of the stage. The Justice of the Peace comes out in his black suit and motions for everyone to stand.

It's time for me to walk into the next phase of my life.

It's hard to remember that I was once a girl who was hidden from the world, who knew nothing, who was scared of her own shadow.

The girl who believed she had no right to ask for anything.

My life has come full circle. The bright lights are gone. The fans. The spectacle. I'm back at the dance academy that first gave me my taste of freedom.

But now I live on *my* terms. Nobody tells me what to think, where to go, how to be. I make my own choices. I have become the person I want to be.

I have chosen this life, my dance, and my husband.

It's time to live it.

And so, I take my first step.

PART 2: SURPRISE

Chapter One

❧

O *ne year later.*

THE CALL COMES MUCH LIKE WE IMAGINED IT would.

Blitz and I are at home, the same house we've always lived in, still rented because the owners won't agree to sell. With our future so uncertain, we haven't been throwing money around like we might have back in the *Dance Blitz* days.

I've just gotten back from four months touring with a small ballet company performing *The Magic Flute*. I only had a small role, but once again, Blitz negotiated recording rights, and several streaming services are interested in airing the production.

We're getting by. Better than getting by. We're happy.

And then comes the call.

Blitz punches *accept* for a Facetime request from his lawyer. Larry appears on the screen.

"Hello Blitz," he says. "Livia."

"Hey Larry," I say. "You have an update?"

"The judge made his ruling."

Blitz and I exchange a glance. We've talked through various scenarios. That the studio will drop the lawsuit. That we'll be able to continue to put off the actual civil trial with delays and injunctions. Or that the lawyers will come to some sort of settlement.

But none of those things have happened. The network canceled the show after Mack's season. The other producers took a giant financial hit. Everyone felt cheated and angry about how the show fizzled without Blitz and our live wedding to save it. We went to trial. And now comes the judge's order.

"Just lay it out," Blitz says.

Larry nods. "First, the good news. The judge ruled the original amount was excessive given how the production overstepped its contract, particularly with Livia. My filing a countersuit on her behalf did mitigate the damage considerably."

"We thank you for that," Blitz says.

"But the damages are substantial. Even if we factored in relinquishing your stake as a producer, the compensation the judge laid out doesn't look good. He agreed the network could demonstrate that refusing to do the televised wedding was a willful breach of contract that prematurely ended the franchise."

Blitz and I exchange another glance as my stomach falls.

"How bad?" I ask.

"Unless we appeal, Blitz is definitely wiped. Looking at the laws of Texas, they can't take your house, but of course, you rent. His Los Angeles condo was always property of the franchise, and it will be sold against damages. All liquid holdings will be seized. Even if we sell everything else, all stocks and bonds and CDs, your financial guys advise me that we're still looking at a shortfall somewhere in the neighborhood of twenty million."

I am stunned quiet. Twenty million in debt. How does anybody ever get out of a hole like that?

Blitz's expression seems unchanged. "So what are my options?"

"Appeal. Bankruptcy. I can file either thing, but be aware that even my retainer is going to run out at the end of the month."

"You've been paid up till now, though, right?"

"Don't worry about that. We work these things out. But that does end pretty much as soon as I file the next round."

"I can pay him," I say.

Larry shakes his head. "Livia's assets should be kept as separate from yours as possible."

"But we're married," I say.

"You weren't when this lawsuit was filed. You are completely out of involvement on this."

Blitz squeezes my hand. "It will be fine. We'll work it out on my side."

I sit back on the sofa. I don't want him to have to work this out alone. But it's not like I have twenty million lying around either. A lot of what I got paid for on the show I went through during my ballet tours. Our need for bodyguards and private floors of hotels for security reasons grossly exceeded the amount I was making as a ballerina.

We no longer live that way, of course, and it isn't necessary now that our fame has dwindled. But I do have some money. We aren't going to go hungry or anything.

Still. Twenty million.

Blitz runs his fingers through his hair. "Do we have any basis to appeal this?"

"Certainly," Larry says. "But, I gotta tell you, Drake Addler has some ideas that I think you might want to listen to."

Drake Addler is one of the four producers of *Dance Blitz*. The nice one.

"Any idea what he's thinking?" Blitz asks.

"Not a clue. He contacted me after the ruling."

"Isn't it too late to negotiate now?"

"He anticipated you might appeal."

"Maybe he doesn't want to drag it out any longer," I venture.

Blitz nods at me. "I'll give him a ring. I'll update you if anything changes."

Larry gives us a salute. "I'll hold off on anything further until we settle out. You two take care."

He ends the call.

Blitz wraps his arm around my waist and drags me closer to him. "I thought we agreed, no deals," he says. "We wanted this behind us no matter what it cost us."

"But it's so much."

I don't know the total of Blitz's assets. His agent originally told us that abandoning the contract would cost sixty-three million, but that was before all the producers, as well as the network, joined the suit.

Blitz closes his eyes, his fingers drifting through my hair. "What have we planned for our near future?" he asks. "Are we doing any traveling?"

"There's only the charity dance in Chicago and hosting some awards ceremony for the ballroom dance organization."

"That's right," he says. "I probably should find some paying gigs."

"I think it would take more than a few gigs to make up the shortfall," I say.

"Don't worry about that figure. It's just a number."

"A really big number."

"These are the sorts of numbers they always throw around."

"We should've bought a house," I say, looking around. "At least it's not expensive to rent this one. I can cover it for a while."

He presses his lips to my hair. "Don't even worry about that, Princess," he says. "We're going to be just fine."

He keeps saying that, but I don't see how. As dancers, there aren't a whole lot of gigs that pay enough to keep you going, even if you were once famous. The only thing that gets you out of a hole like we're in right now is the one thing we've been trying to avoid—fame.

Chapter Two

※

Our names jump into the news again as word of the judge's ruling hits the entertainment sites. Reporters and photographers appear at the end of our street, but we manage to get away. Rather than holing up somewhere expensive, we ditch Blitz's Jaguar at a fancy hotel as a decoy and take my white Volkswagen convertible back to Blitz's parents' house.

Renata is there with freshly made tamales.

We ride out the publicity storm with home cooking and reruns of old westerns, a favorite of Blitz's father.

Blitz's brother Dante comes to visit, ribbing Blitz about his fall from grace. We spend several easy evenings on the family's back porch, eating Renata's endless rounds of cooking while the two boys take good-natured jabs at each other.

"What about you?" Blitz asks his brother. "You staying in that dead-end job?"

Dante kicks back in the swivel chair, a glass dangling from his fingertips. He's a couple of years younger than Blitz, but with a more devilish attitude. It's clear the brothers have a good relationship, although we haven't spent a lot of time together between my ballet schedule and Dante's work in New York.

"So being a CEO is a dead-end job?" Dante asks. He squints one eye at Blitz.

"Nothing but sitting at a desk," Blitz says.

"At least I don't work in tights."

"Touché."

We stare across the yard as the stars come out. It's late summer and the cicadas are loud enough to drown out the sounds of traffic.

Dante peers into the sky. "Can't see shit for stars from my uptown loft," he says.

"Who needs stars when you have Times Square?" Blitz asks.

"You like it in New York?" I ask him.

"Love it. But it's nice to come here and kick back."

We're quiet for a bit, listening to an errant toad that has made its way into the backyard to try his luck with the ladies at the koi pond in the back corner of the fence.

A queasiness settles in my belly. Probably too much grease. The delicious but heavy Mexican food Renata has treated us to since we've been staying at her house is finally getting to me. I'll have to cut back, stick to salads. We definitely don't have a fitness chef anymore.

I sip ice water laced with wedges of lime and try not to worry. Drake Addler will come up with something, I believe in that. He is one of the few people on the *Dance Blitz* team we can trust.

I feel sleepy as Blitz and Dante's voices lower to murmurs. Everything will work out. It has to.

I WAKE UP WITH A START SOMETIME LATER. THE queasiness is much more than a turn in my belly. Much, much more.

Blitz and Dante have moved away, walking the circumference of the yard and talking quietly.

I jump from the chair and rush inside. Blitz calls out after me, but I wave him off. "Just going in for a second!"

I barely make it to the bathroom by the guest room before I throw up in the toilet.

I did eat four tamales. Never again.

I sit on the floor a while, my head resting on the cool edge of the bathtub.

This is a long way from my lowest low, given where I've been in my twenty-two years. But it sure feels like the lowest point in a while.

The threat of bankruptcy, hiding at my husband's family home, the talk of everyone, and not in a good way. And now overeating. I can definitely stand for this period of my life to be over.

When it feels safe enough to stand up and walk, I splash some water on my face and head to our bedroom. David likes his house cold, and the air brushing against my face from the vents is calming and blissfully cool.

I slide between the sheets, not even bothering to change. It's been a long few days. I just need some sleep.

And to eat some vegetables.

Chapter Three

꧁❦꧂

When I wake up the next morning, Blitz is already up.

I can tell he's been there by the impression in his pillow and the tousle of the sheet on his side.

I listen to the sounds of the house for a moment, trying to determine what might be happening. The television is on, and the gunfire coming from the speakers means David is watching another western.

The clicking sound of flip-flops tells me Renata is moving around the house. But no matter how long I listen, I don't catch Blitz's voice, or his brother's.

I sit up on the edge of the bed when nausea hits me again.

What?

I hurry out the door and across the hall to the

bathroom. I barely make it inside before I upchuck again.

Terrified that someone is going to hear me being sick, and Renata worrying that her cooking caused it, I quickly turn on all the faucets to drown out the sound.

This time, however, there isn't really anything to come up. I spit a few times, trying to puzzle it out. Then an icy thread of understanding bolts through me.

I've felt this before.

Seven years ago.

I'm pregnant.

The last few months run through my mind.

Going on tour, and forgetting to see my OB/GYN before I left.

Running out of pill packets, but not worrying about it because Blitz wasn't on tour with me.

Intending to get right back on it when I came back, but then Blitz good-naturedly saying condoms were fine for a while.

And then all this stuff with the lawsuit.

Those first few times after I'd returned, we hadn't used any protection at all.

That was about a few weeks ago.

Oh no.

The only thing that flashes through my mind is the number *twenty million*. Twenty million dollars.

How can we have a baby when we are being sued for twenty million dollars more than we have? My neck breaks out in a cold sweat. This cannot be happening.

I'm about to start throwing up again when suddenly a wave of calm washes over me. My breathing slows, and the nausea slips away.

I'm going to have a baby. Blitz's baby. I'll get to be a mom again. Gabriella will have a brother or sister.

I can already picture a little boy just like Blitz, funny and cute and silly and smart.

Will he be a dancer too?

But what if it's a girl? Will she look like Gabriella? With Blitz's Hispanic features, she'll certainly have the same black hair.

We can do this.

Blitz managed to resurrect his career from the media graveyard. He can do anything, and together, the two of us are unstoppable. We've proven that.

I flush the toilet, turning off all the faucets. The nausea has calmed down, although I sense it lying in wait for next time. I've been through this before. I can handle it. And it will be so different. Nothing could possibly be harder than the way I had to endure a pregnancy last time.

Blitz is right, of course. Twenty million is just a number. It could be two hundred million, or a trillion. All that really matters is that we can get through each day.

Isn't that what bankruptcy is for? It just erases that stupid amount of money they're trying to insist they take from us. It shouldn't even be theirs. They didn't do the work, the rehearsals, the dancing, and the appearances. We did.

And then what? Our credit is wrecked? We can't get a loan? So what. We'll work for a living like everyone else. We'll live paycheck to paycheck. We'll pay in cash.

I brush my teeth and wash my face, then look at myself in the mirror.

"You're going to be a mother again," I say. The face looking back at me certainly is older and wiser than the last one who peered out with a baby on the way.

I'm strong now. And I have a team. I won't have to do any of this alone.

My life has been amazing for several years.

This is the next perfect step.

Now, I just need to tell Blitz.

Chapter Four

When Blitz returns from golfing with his brother, I don't get a single chance to talk to him alone. More friends come over. More food arrives. I smile and hang onto him, hoping the nausea stays under control.

The gathering becomes a house party. We see the real estate agent who helped us look for a house before I left for my first ballet tour. And the owner of the Mexican restaurant where Blitz and I had our first official date.

It's like a reunion. I move happily from room to room with Blitz, and carefully stick to simple foods with the least amount of grease as possible.

At times I think I will spring it on him in front of everyone—I'm pregnant! What a party it would be then.

But I haven't taken a test. What if I'm wrong?

The next morning, when Blitz is sleeping off the late night, I slip out and head to a drug store. I almost laugh at my secrecy, the scarf and sunglasses, worried someone will recognize me and start a Twitter storm about Blitz's wife buying a pregnancy test.

But I'm not seen, and the cashier doesn't even look me in the face as she scans the test and absently accepts my cash.

I hole up in the guest bathroom to pee on the stick. I wonder if I should get Blitz up and take it together, but I'm so afraid of being wrong. I don't want to make a big deal if it's just bad eating choices or a nervous stomach over the lawsuit.

I sit on the floor and stare at the stick where it rests on the side of the bathtub. The wetness inches across the window, and instantly a plus sign shows in the oval.

It's positive.

I'm really pregnant.

Another baby is already inside me.

I press my hands to my belly, overwhelmed by every emotion coursing through me.

I'm going to be a mom a second time.

What will Blitz say when I tell him? Will he be excited? Or worried about our future?

I hide the stick away in my makeup bag and sneak

back to our room. Blitz still sleeps, oblivious to this huge change taking place. I slide next to him and put my arms around his waist. My husband. The father of my baby. It's so different this time, so wonderful compared to the fear and horror and shame I felt as a teen with an unexpected pregnancy with a boy I no longer knew.

When Blitz shows no sign of waking, I shift away, holding my phone with the screen angled away from him and earphones silencing the audio. I watch video after video of women telling their husbands they are pregnant with all manner of signage, singing telegrams, or just opening a box with the test inside.

And that's when I get an idea that might solve all our problems.

JULIET CLAREMONT AND HER HUSBAND BENNETT meet me at a quiet tea shop on San Antonio's east side the next day.

The two of them founded Dreamcatcher Dance Academy for Juliet's mother when she had cancer. They were instrumental in helping me when Blitz and I were first together, and I trust them completely. As a bonus, Bennett was once one of the primary producers of *Dance Blitz,* before he sold his stake to Blitz, so he understands the business we're in.

I choose a tea shop on purpose because I remember from my last pregnancy how certain scents can set me off, and a sandwich shop seems the least risky.

Still, as I slide into a chair opposite Bennett and Juliet, the smells assault me. Tuna fish. Strong cheese. I don't think I'll be able to eat more than a bit of toast.

Juliet looks beautiful in a white sundress with pale watercolor flowers cascading down one side. Apparently, the heat, combined with the fact that it's a Saturday afternoon, has convinced Bennett to ditch the full suit, and he is as casual as anyone ever sees him in sharply pressed khakis and a pale-blue button-down.

"It's so lovely to see you," Juliet says, reaching out to squeeze my arm. "How was your ballet season?"

"Grueling," I say.

Juliet laughs. "I think that's the first thing we all say when we're not speaking to donors and patrons."

"It's a lovely ballet," I say. "But I'll be happy to never try twenty-seven pirouettes in a row again."

Bennett leans forward, his hands clasped on the table like he's about to conduct a board meeting. "You have plans for another tour?"

I hesitate. "Not quite yet."

A jolly middle-aged woman with fading pink hair approaches the table. "I'm not going to pay any attention to the fact that you're famous," she says. "I sense you're nervous about that."

"Thank you," I say.

She bends over to whisper, "We cater to an older crowd. They probably won't notice."

Great. Maybe I should have chosen someplace completely private, like the dance studio or Juliet's house, for this conversation.

"Can I have iced tea with lemon?" I ask.

"Certainly, my dear. What about you two?"

Bennett and Juliet place orders for drinks and a round of scones. I'm relieved they've kept their food simple because even the smell of sugar is beginning to get to me.

"I'd like to think you wanted to see us to say hello," Juliet says, "but I have a feeling you have something particular on your mind."

I fiddle with the edges of the pink linen napkin on the table in front of me. I don't want to tell someone else my secret before I tell Blitz, and I have practiced a thousand different ways to say this. But as the words are about to leave my mouth, I'm not sure of any of them anymore.

"I guess you know about the lawsuit," I say.

Bennett sits back in this chair. "I do. It's outrageous. Blitz's counsel is good, though. Has there been a development since the ruling?"

"No. Well, other than Drake Addler having some

suggestions for Blitz that we don't know about yet."

"He's probably going to pitch some sort of spinoff for Blitz in order to take the hounds off the lawsuit," Bennett says. "If Blitz goes back into a contract with the shareholders, he can make settling the suit a contingency."

"We don't really want to go back into the public eye," I say. Then I realize, well that's silly, given what I'm thinking of doing. "But I guess we need to look at options."

"Blitz can file for bankruptcy," Bennett says. "It's not as uncommon as you might think, to shed one business and start another."

I've never thought of our careers as a business, but I guess he's right.

"What if I had a bit of newsworthy information about us, something so big it would be worth a lot of money? How would I best go about...selling it?"

Bennett and Juliet pass a look between them.

"It's good news," I say. "Nothing bad. I just feel like it could do something. It's big, no one knows other than me, and it seems like an opportunity."

The woman returns with the drinks as well as scones and a caddy of jams. "Anything else?" she asks.

"We're good, thank you," Juliet says.

We all wait until she is well away before we speak again.

Bennett wraps his hands around a glass. "If this

news is what I suspect it is, are you saying Blitz doesn't know?"

"That's right. I've been watching videos showing wives breaking the news, and it seems like this could be big, the sort of thing talk shows live for."

"Let me make some inquiries," Bennett says. "Are you thinking about surprising him on a national news show? Because we could probably get a bidding war going." He taps his finger on the rim of his glass. "But I'd hesitate to let too many people know, in case it's leaked and wrecks the whole deal."

Juliet sets plates in front of each of us. "Is that what you had in mind, Livia? A news show?"

"I honestly don't know. It just seems if something can rack up fifty million views on social media, it has to be worth something. I want to milk it for all it's worth, given our situation. Larry said to keep Blitz's assets separate, so if all this revenue was mine then we could keep it, even with the lawsuit."

"Yes," Bennett says. "We would want to establish something in your name only to make sure it isn't accessible by the creditors," Bennett says. "And we should do that first. And it should probably happen quickly, right? It might be hard to keep the secret."

"That's where I think the Drake Addler thing comes in," I say. "If I can send Blitz away for a week of meetings, then he won't notice."

Juliet sits up straight. "But you'll be alone with all

this ugliness in the press right now."

"I can stay with Blitz's parents," I say.

"Are they able to keep the secret? What if they notice?"

"They're not nosy," I say. "And they're used to Blitz's fame. I'd go back to our house, but I'm afraid there will be reporters there as long as the lawsuit is a popular topic."

Juliet turns to Bennett. "What if she stays with us? That way she's close for any deals we're negotiating on her behalf, and there's no concern that someone will overhear." She tilts her head meaningfully at the waitress, who seems to be making closer passes than necessary as she carries dishes to other tables.

"I think we will table this discussion for now," Bennett says. "And I agree. Let's get Drake to pull Blitz away. We'll use ballet as an excuse to get Livia to our house. And then try to negotiate something within the next seven days."

I take a scone from the platter and break off a tiny bite. My stomach is already settling. I'm doing the right thing. No matter what happens with the lawsuit, if I can raise a decent amount of money on my own, then we will be all right through the pregnancy and the birth of the baby even if I can't work as a ballerina.

It feels good to have a plan.

Chapter Five

The timing works out perfectly.

I tell Blitz about Juliet's invitation to do some intense ballet study at her private studio on the Claremont estate. Within an hour of this conversation, Drake Addler calls Blitz to see if he can fly to L.A. to discuss this idea he has.

Blitz suggests he goes alone to meet Drake so I can study with Juliet. He thinks it's *his* idea. We couldn't have planned it better.

Meanwhile, I've been desperately trying to hide my toilet hugging from everyone.

When David leaves to take Blitz to the airport, Renata pops into the bedroom as I pack my ballet clothes and a few other items to take to Juliet's.

She sits on the bed. "It was so nice having you and Benjamin here for a while."

I continue folding leotards and stacking them in a suitcase. It's hard to meet my mother-in-law's eyes. I'm afraid she'll see how sick I feel and will guess the reason.

I'm not sure I could explain my reasons for keeping the news from Blitz. We haven't let his parents in on the extent of the financial hardship of the lawsuit. They believe, like most people do, that it's simply an annoying legal matter.

I turn to the dresser, willing my stomach to calm down. I sort through a drawer as I say, "It's been so lovely being here. A nice escape from all the publicity."

I sense Renata hesitating at whatever she wants to say next, so I set down the stack of legwarmers I've been gathering and turn around.

"Is everything okay?" I ask.

Renata smiles at me, but her eyes remain full of concern. "I know this terrible lawsuit must be a great strain on you. I want you and Blitz to know that no matter what happens, you always have a home here."

So she's guessed it's bigger than we've said.

I sit down beside her. "I don't think it will be that bad. If nothing else, I've made money along the way. And we have our rather famous names we can always fall back on."

I borrow a line from Bennett. "Our careers are

like a business. Sometimes you have to close one location so you can open a new one."

"It sounds like you have good advisors," she says. "And I can't pretend to understand how all this works. I just wanted you to know you're welcome here."

I reach over and give her a tight hug. "I know, and I'm thankful."

She speaks against my hair. "I know things haven't always been perfect with your family. I can't understand how parents could treat their child as they did. But that is not the case with us."

My eyes squeeze tight. Even though my relationship with my mother has been repaired, and I get to see my brother whenever I like, it's true the rift with my father will never go away.

I'm not sure that it should. The things he said to me, and the way I was hidden away for so much of my life, can never be undone. I will carry the lingering shame with me always.

I pull away from Renata. "Blitz will be back in a few days," I say. "Maybe we can plan a nice dinner for all of us. We're hoping this dies down if no new information is leaked to the tabloids."

"That sounds lovely. Maybe the new Thai place that opened in the shopping center down the street?"

The very thought of spicy food or peanut sauce makes my belly turn over, so I quickly return to my drawers, willing my stomach to stay settled. Only when I am sure my voice will work correctly do I say, "That might be nice."

Mercifully, a timer dings in the kitchen, and Renata hurries out of the room. She's barely disappeared down the hall before I dash to the bathroom and turn the water on full blast to cover the sound of my retching.

It's a good thing I'm leaving today. With Blitz gone, Renata is sure to interact with me more. There is no way I can hide this for long.

Chapter Six

The days on the Claremont estate pass quickly. Juliet and I manage to practice some light ballet. I never tell her straight out that I'm pregnant, still unwilling to say the words aloud until I say them to Blitz. But I'm sure Juliet has guessed. I've thrown up a million times, everywhere from the guest bathrooms to the rose bushes.

I call my doctor but use a fake name, concerned someone might see the records and spill the news. I explain I'm a pregnant dancer and ask about continuing my ballet work.

The nurse is great, as always, and assures me my workouts can continue as long as they are not aggressive and I don't overstretch, since the tendons will loosen up as the pregnancy progresses. She tells me to monitor my heart rate and exertion levels.

When she transfers me to the appointment desk for my first exam, I hang up. I will go in soon, but the last thing I want to do is alert some random clerk that a famous baby is on the way. Not while we're working a deal.

Blitz calls to video chat every day, and occasionally I have to deny the call, pretending to be in the middle of a workout when I'm really throwing up my guts.

It turns out Drake Addler is indeed pitching a dance talent show for Blitz, and the irony of it all is that it focuses on young talent instead of adult couples. Blitz has no idea he's about to become the ideal father-figure host. It will be a complete turnaround of his reputation if he does it.

About four days later, Juliet and I are sipping lemonade on the back patio when Bennett comes home with an update.

He loosens his tie and sits next to Juliet. "So here's where we stand. I did a general call for proposals with the promise of exclusive news about you and Blitz to the highest bidder. I took the three bids my media people considered to be the most credible and safe. We sent a nondisclosure agreement that would scare the pants off of anybody, with fines up to three million dollars for the leak of the information."

"Do we have to go with the highest bidder?" Juliet asks.

"No. I'm not going to do an auction. I want Livia to see the bids and the proposed media outlets."

"What are the choices?" I ask.

Bennett opens a folder and turns it around so I can see it.

"First is a morning news show, sort of what you first envisioned. You can see the viewer numbers, who would be interviewing you, and the format. The second is an entertainment cable station. They are pitching something more elaborate, a retrospective on the show with your news being the culmination."

"Do they know what the news is yet?" Juliet asks.

"No, we'll do that in the final bidding session to delay the possibility of a leak," Bennett says. "The third one is a print tabloid. They are seeking a cover image, as well as the right to sell spinoff stories to help recoup some of the cost. That might be the least invasive because there's no video, just print."

"Print will have less of a splash, though, won't it?" I ask. "I'm ready to go all out. Merchandising. The whole thing."

Bennett chuckles. "We'll make a media mogul out of you yet."

Juliet turns to me. "What do you think, Livia? Do you want to be interviewed on the television show, or would you rather just do a photo shoot and a print interview?"

"I want to be everywhere at once," I say.

"Then I'll speak with the two broadcast offers," Bennett says. "We might make a secondary deal with the first bump pictures. Those are all the rage."

Juliet leans forward and presses her hands over Bennett's. "You know, Livia hasn't told us what this news is, exactly."

Bennett gives a brief nod. "Of course. I don't know a thing about anyone throwing up behind the bales of hay in one of the empty horse stalls."

My face blooms hot. "I'm so sorry."

He holds up his hands. "It's all right. The horses do much worse. But it's good you're secluded. If you go out in public at all, the news will be out before we want it to."

"How much control do we have over what they air?"

"I can get as tight a contract on them as I want," Bennett says, "I can ask for preapproval and every-thing. But ultimately, we do not control how the story gets out after the broadcast. The second wave of news can pitch it any way they want, and they will. They'll try to differentiate themselves as the news goes from exclusive to mainstream."

"What do you think they'll say?" I ask.

"Anything could happen, but that would be the

case whether we control the opening salvo or not. Someone will inevitably question paternity. Any man you've danced with will be in question for those who want to be salacious. Just know what you're up against, find a good place to lie low, and make sure your appearances after the news is out are strategic and controlled."

Julia sets down her glass. "Speaking of controlled, how are we going to keep it from leaking early just based on who's there when she tells Blitz?"

"That I can truly control," Bennett says. "We will be using my secure offices."

Juliet nods in approval. "Excellent. Nobody gets past your doors if you don't want them to."

I settle back on the cushioned chair. At least this is done. I trust Bennett to get me the best deal and the easiest experience. We can talk later about potentially selling sonograms, maternity clothes fittings, whatever I need to do to keep us afloat while we get out from under the lawsuit.

"You're going to be right up there with the royal babies," I tell my belly.

"That's a fact," Bennett says. "And an excellent point. I'll call someone in London security to see how they manage the whole famous baby bit. We're going to need all the ideas we can get when you go into labor."

Labor. Delivery. I hadn't even thought past this first part, the throwing up and telling Blitz.

My last hospital experience had been horrific. I can only hope that with a husband, support staff, and a few more years of life under my belt, this one will be beautiful and lovely.

I want that for my baby. But also, I want it for me.

Chapter Seven

In the week Blitz is gone, Juliet and I try everything to figure out how to get control of this morning sickness. We consult with a private physician who works with Bennett and can ensure confidentiality. He assures me my level of nausea is normal, and to just avoid things that will trigger it; an empty stomach, intense smells, and getting overtired, which lowers my threshold to manage anything.

This is nothing I couldn't have learned off the Internet.

Still, we make sure I wake up to crackers and juice, and the Claremont cook indulges me by bringing various types of food into the room to see if it triggers my nausea, so we know what to avoid when Blitz returns.

Bacon is definitely the worse. Almost instant puking.

His mother makes bacon every morning.

The interview and photo shoots will be recorded the day after he gets back. All I have to do is hide it from him for twenty-four hours.

We have Blitz come to the Claremont estate to meet me. The environment is carefully controlled here, and I don't have to worry about his mother cooking something that might set me off. There are also many more rooms and large spaces to rattle around in, and both Juliet and Bennett have promised to steer him away should I give the signal that I need to escape.

If all else fails, we're pretty sure we can play the whole thing off as a tummy bug until the actual interview. Juliet is prepared with a story that she just got over a stomach virus and she hopes it wasn't contagious.

When Blitz walks into the sunroom, where Juliet and I are chatting about a ballet video we just watched, I am more relieved to see him than I expected.

Emotions spring to me more suddenly than before, and when I stand to greet him, I hug him extra tight and long.

He kisses my hair. "I think a certain princess missed me."

I nod against his shoulder. I want to blurt the news out right then, be alone with him, and talk through everything I've been feeling, including what I can't say to Juliet. About the flashbacks of my first pregnancy I've been having. How sometimes I wake up thinking my father is standing over my bed, his arms crossed in anger. That sometimes I hear an infant's cry when the house is quiet, and this unsettled feeling that this baby will be taken away from me, too, sets off a round of torrential crying.

As all these thoughts swirl through me, Blitz, as always, senses that I'm off.

"Hey. What's wrong, baby?"

When I can't gather myself together enough to answer, he turns to Juliet. But she simply says, "I'll give you two some time," and slips away.

Blitz drops onto a cushioned wicker loveseat and pulls me onto his lap. I steel myself to get some control and pull away to look him in the eyes. "It's always harder being away from you when the paparazzi are after us," I say. I pray that's enough excuse for him.

His shoulders relax. "Have you been trapped here?"

"Pretty much. Juliet and I watched some ballets and did lots of workouts. It's been fun. But I've definitely missed you. And Ted." Our bodyguard and

177

driver went back to his old job when we tightened our budget.

"Well, if this thing with Drake works out, we will be able to bring him on again."

"Tell me all about it. Tell me everything."

As Blitz outlines Drake's plan for a kid dance show pilot, I do a quick self-assessment. Tears dried up? Stomach settled? Secret safe?

I sure hope so.

THE MORNING OF THE TAPING, I'M A NERVOUS wreck. We've chosen my best time of day for the recording session, when I'm least likely to throw up. Bennett has spirited Blitz away for a round of golf at a very exclusive club, ensuring that Blitz will be well dressed for the interview without arousing suspicion when Bennett suggests he shouldn't wear workout clothes.

It also gets him out of the house while the makeup and hair teams arrive to give me just the right look for a famous mother-to-be.

We settle on long, loose curls and extremely natural makeup with pink accents.

My dress is silky pale-blue, my signature color on the show, one that reflects back to the first days I knew Blitz and would wear my one good leotard.

Juliet brings me a pair of pale-blue ballet toe shoes. I will do a photo or two as a ballerina, and we will auction off the shoes for a children's charity afterword for additional positive publicity. This was my idea, hoping to counteract any negative things that might be said about Blitz or me, or any trouble the former contestants might stir up to get themselves back in the headlines.

We've been through all this before. I can predict some of the directions people will go once Blitz and I hit the magazine covers again.

When I'm put together, Bennett sends a private car for me, and Juliet and I head to his office.

When we enter the spacious conference room, I'm not sure if I'm late or they're early, but a cluster of people are standing amidst the cameras and lights, waiting for something to happen.

A young woman in a flowing black tunic is the first to rush over.

"Livia Mays," she says, using my stage name. "It's such an honor to be interviewing you today."

She must be Blaine, the host of the show. She seems younger than when I see her on camera, not that I've watched it a lot.

Several others approach. One of them is an older woman in a dark-gray pantsuit. She has a hard edge about her, something about the pinch of her mouth or the wrinkles between her eyes. I'm guessing she's from the network, as she has that "I'm in charge of all of you" look.

"I love your dress," Blaine says. "It's the exact shade of blue everyone knows you in."

I give her a nod. It no longer surprises me that people know my signature color or the style of clothes I typically wear. At the height of my fame with Blitz, every outfit I wore and hairstyle I chose was dissected by the entertainment sites.

I still have no idea why this is so interesting. Or why my being pregnant is such a valuable scoop. I suppose readers like to live vicariously through celebrities. While it's normally one of the side effects of fame I find difficult, today, I admit I'm glad I can use it to my advantage.

"This is Juliet Claremont," I say to Blaine. "She's a very close friend of mine."

Juliet extends a hand to shake Blaine's. The network woman still hasn't approached us, or the crew.

"So Blaine," I say, "have you been told what's happening here today? It's been held a secret."

At this, the woman in the suit comes forward. She has a no-nonsense stride like she is commanding the room. "We're about to inform them," she says.

Blaine's false smile freezes in place as the woman shakes my hand as if this is someone she has to endure.

"I'm Martha Gimble," the woman says. "I'm the executive producer of Mornings with Bea and Blaine. "We appreciate you trusting your important moment to us."

At that, Blaine's eyes grow big. "What important moment?" She turns to me. "Is this more than an interview?

A murmur goes through the crew.

I glance at Martha. I know the drill. She's the boss. "Are we going to tell them in advance?" I'm still not committed to saying the words aloud.

Martha turns to the group clustered in the corner. They all look to be camera operators and lighting crew. "All right, everyone, gather close."

Blaine's eyes are wide with excitement. No doubt visions of audience ratings are dancing through her head. I don't miss her glancing at my belly. Martha was right to withhold information. It's too easy to figure out.

"I will remind everyone in this room that you all signed confidentiality agreements. I need everyone to remove their cell phones from their pockets and hand them to me." Martha holds out a black-and-gold Michael Kors tote. "I'll return them to you when this recording has ended."

I glance over at Juliet, who shrugs. They're making sure nobody has footage but them. This stuff would probably be worth a small fortune if they could sneak a quick shot. I should know. I'm being paid for it.

"When is this going to air?" I ask.

"In the morning," Martha says as the crew drops their phones into her bag. "I picked my best people for this, but that doesn't mean they won't be tempted."

I'm glad I'll have time to call my mom and Blitz's parents before the footage airs. One of the reasons not to do a live show was to make sure the right people heard first.

Martha closes the bag and slings it over her shoulder. "Any leak of what is about to happen," she says to the crew, "means every single one of you is fired and you will all be named in an immediate breach of contract suit." She makes eye contact with each person. "I assure you there is no payment you could be made for a Tweet, an interview, or any break of confidentiality that would cover what the network would do to you."

Her eyes sweep the room again. "And furthermore, don't even breathe of it to your wives, your girlfriends, or your mothers. Not until after 8 a.m. Eastern, when the world will be talking about what happened here and sharing the footage you took."

She puts on a stiff smile. "Be proud of your work here. It's going to be the most viral thing since a Kardashian broke the Internet."

The crew glances at each other, the excitement building. This is clearly not normal protocol for them.

I decide to step in and soften Martha's harshness with my own touch.

"I'm so grateful you're all here," I say. "I trust you with this secret with all my heart. Today, in less than an hour, my husband Blitz Craven is going to enter this room thinking he's stepping into a photo shoot for my ballet work. But instead, I will be telling him something truly amazing." Instead of saying what the news is, I press my hands to my belly.

Now the gasps begin. Blaine smiles knowingly. One of the crewmembers covers her mouth, eyes wide.

"He has no idea. We've kept the secret so that it can be revealed on your show. With your beautiful work."

"Will you dance?" asks a young man with a lightning bolt shaved into the side of his head.

"Maybe? I'm not sure how he's going to react."

"Do we have music?" another man asks.

"You have music," Martha says. "Trevon will be directing. He'll give you the potential shot list now."

An energetic man in a black tracksuit begins passing out a stapled script to everyone.

"Oh, Livia!" A woman with an explosion of curls

hurries forward. She envelops me in a tight apricot-shampoo-smelling hug. "I'm so happy for you."

With that, everyone rushes forward to congratulate me. As much as I love their enthusiasm, I feel overwhelmed by hairspray, perfumes, and body lotion. I have to clench my jaw to keep my nausea level as under control as possible.

Eventually, Martha gets their attention. "Let me remind you we still have lighting tests to do! Everyone, places!"

I'm terribly relieved to be free of their closeness, and newly grateful that Juliet and Bennett have such subtle scents.

Trevon steps in front of the crew. "We'll rehearse with a stand-in for Blitz. We don't know how the moment will actually unfold, but I want to be prepared for anything. Give yourself plenty of space in case he picks her up or walks in circles or whatever he might do."

I've thought about this moment a million times. I'm not exactly sure how Blitz will react. He'll probably come in for a hug. He might whisper something only I can hear. But Blitz is a showman of the highest order. Even if he falters for a second, he will instinctively know to milk the moment for all of its television worth.

At least, I think he will. He could be blindsided. I'm sure he'll be happy. My heart flutters just thinking about it. He's about to know. This secret I've carried for a week will finally be out.

"All right," Trevon says. "Let's get some footage for the promo spots. Livia, Blaine will guide you through it. If for some reason we don't get everything we need before he arrives, we can always run more afterward."

"Maybe," Juliet says. "Her hair and makeup might change depending on what Blitz does during his reaction."

"Good point," Trevon says. "Let's get on it."

I step onto the set with Blaine. She is tiny, and despite having always been on the small side, I feel like I tower over her. Lights are adjusted, cameras shift up and down.

I can't wait to see the wonder on his face. Moments like this don't come along very often.

When everything seems set, Blaine faces the camera and waits for the cue from Trevon.

"Hello. This is Blaine Adams with Mornings with Bea and Blaine. I'm here with Livia Mays, who you remember from her two seasons of *Dance Blitz* with her now-husband Blitz Craven." She turns to me. "I'm so glad you could be here with us, Livia."

"Thank you for bringing me on," I say. Gone are the nerves I once felt on television or in interviews. It has become second nature. Even though this is a particularly unique situation, it will be handled with kid gloves. This is not a gotcha interview or a scenario where someone will try to trick me into saying something to increase the ratings.

It's a heavily curated and carefully considered once-in-a-lifetime moment.

"I understand something special is happening today," Blaine continues. "Can you tell us about it?"

I give the camera a shy smile. "We're waiting for Blitz to get here. We have some amazing news for our fans."

Blaine's interview goes on for a while, then Trevon stops us, adjusts the lights, and we start again. It's comfortable and easy at first, but as we near closer to when Blitz will arrive, my nerves begin to rattle. My stomach roils with nausea, and suddenly I'm terribly afraid I'm going to throw up.

Panic overwhelms me. We didn't bring a spare dress. How could we have forgotten that? What if I throw up on this one? What if Blitz walks in, and I'm on the floor, puking my guts up? How will I get the words out? What sort of moment will be recorded for posterity?

"Livia?" Blaine asks, and it seems like it might not be the first time. "Are you okay?"

"Grab a chair," Juliet commands. "I hope you have your lights set because she needs to rest."

A flurry of activity surrounds me. A chair is brought over. A cup of water.

Juliet kneels beside me. "How are you doing? Should I fetch a trash can?"

I shake my head. And this does feel different. It's not like normal nausea, which starts with an acid feeling, and then the vomiting begins.

This is more like I've been sucker punched.

"I think it's just nerves," I say, but when Juliet offers her hand, I clutch it.

"Try some of the things we do before we go out on stage," Juliet says. "The breathing that connects your mind and body. Let the air go in a circle, in your nose, down through your lungs, and back out your mouth."

Her voice is soothing, and I do as she says, carefully breathing with intention.

After a moment I feel more in control. "I'm sorry to be such a diva," I tell the crew.

They laugh it off. Trevon assures me I'm a total dream to work with.

Martha commands them to keep a chair nearby, and stand-ins can do the rest of the lighting tests. I watch from the side of the staging area, my hand to my chest. I have to calm down.

Juliet stands in for me as they block out when Blitz will arrive from the side door, how he will probably hesitate and watch until he's called over. One of the young men of the crew pretends to be Blitz and walks in with exaggerated swagger that makes everyone laugh.

I feel much calmer.

Juliet glances down unexpectedly and pulls her phone from the tiny purse dangling from her wrist. She taps something out quickly.

"Is it him?" Blaine asks.

She nods. "They just got in the elevator."

"Places everyone," Trevon says. "This is the real deal." He turns to me. "Livia, are you up for standing center stage again?"

"I am."

One of the crewmembers comes forward with a still camera as if we are doing the ballet photo shoot as Blitz expects. I haven't warmed up properly to do en pointe, and at this point, I'm not going to risk injuring myself by doing it even for a picture. But I do work my way through standard ballet positions, occasionally coming to demi-pointe, keeping my hands and arms pretty.

The photographer snaps some shots, and when the side door opens, everything is what Blitz expects.

My stomach turns over again. Stay calm. *This is it.*

Blitz wears neatly pressed khakis and a blue collared shirt. He looks handsome and sun-kissed and perfect.

He and Bennett stand to one side, watching the photographs.

As we rehearse, Blaine approaches and shakes his hand. "Would you like a few photographs with your wife?" she asks.

But when Blitz sees her, he catches on instantly. "Aren't you the host of that big morning show?"

Blaine seems to have prepared for this question. "I am. It's wonderful to meet you. My producer said I should come today to approach you guys about a potential spot on our show. I hope you don't mind. The photographer is a friend of mine and he may have tipped me off."

Blitz shakes his head, but he's smiling. "We're hard to catch these days. I'm impressed."

I continue with the photos as if I don't want to waste the photographer's time, but then he lowers his camera. I take that as my cue to say, "Blitz, do you want to take a few with you in them?"

But Blitz holds up a hand. "I'm happy to watch from the sidelines. This is all about you."

Blitz is being humble. This is a contingency we didn't plan for.

But I should have known. He's always been happy to step aside and let me take the limelight.

It's the photographer who saves the day. "I have a kiss image on my shot list," he says. "Should I get a stand-in?"

That gets Blitz moving. "I know when I'm beaten," he says. "Of course I will do the kiss shot with my beautiful wife."

The room relaxes as Blitz finally strides onto the staging area. I hold out my arms for him. This is the moment. The one I have planned for, with Bennett and Juliet's help.

Blitz steps close, sliding his hand up the back of my neck into my hair. There's half a can of hairspray there to tangle his fingers, but he's a professional, and he's used to handling my stage hair. He still acts as if it is soft and sleek.

"You look amazing," he says.

Our stage kisses are well practiced, having been directed a million times over. We know how to position our hands, our bodies, and our heads for the maximum impact and camera angle.

Blitz does this now, and even though it's a staged kiss, one we've done for hundreds of cameras, I know he senses something different about me. It's in the way his lips shift against mine when they would normally hold their position. It's how his hand squeezes my waist, even though that would crinkle the dress for the shot.

He pulls away and looks me in the eyes. "Is everything okay, Princess?"

I draw in a deep breath. We're in the perfect position, our faces just inches away, bodies angled perfectly.

This is show business at its best right here.

But it's also our moment.

"I have something to tell you, Blitz." I pause, knowing the promos for this moment will want to cut there, and I need to give it space.

It's a funny thing, to have a moment so personal and perfect, so life changing and emotional, also be something I have to think about from a production angle. I am trying to save our skins.

But it's also all about us. All *three* of us.

The room is so silent you can actually hear the tick of the hot lights as the metal around the bulbs expands.

He grips me a little tighter. "What is it?"

Normally Blitz would tease me right now, offer some wild suggestions to bring out a laugh. It's the showman in him.

But not today. He seems to understand this is different.

"I'm pregnant," I say. "You're going to be a father."

His eyes widen for a moment as he takes this in. He pulls away and looks down at my belly. "Here?" His hand flattens across my stomach.

"Yes," I say with a smile in my voice.

He looks up at me again, then down at my belly again. "Really?"

"Really," I say.

"When?"

"The baby will arrive in March."

He leans in and bestows another quick kiss on my mouth. "Livia. This is amazing. This is... I can't..."

He kneels down in front of me and holds his cheek to my belly. "Are you in there?"

He presses a kiss into my stomach. "We are going to have the most wonderful life," he says. "You can be anyone you want to be."

He looks up at me. "You're going to have to teach me how to do this," he says.

I slide my hand through his hair. "I think we'll be just like everybody else and figure it out together."

Several moments pass as we take each other in, then from somewhere, the opening notes of a song begin to play. It's one we know well, "The Dream-catcher's Waltz."

I don't know who is playing it, or how, but Juliet is probably behind it. She's the one who would know. The Dreamcatcher's Waltz is what caused Dream-catcher Dance Academy to open in the first place. Where I would take lessons. Where Blitz went when times got hard. It's where we met.

He stands and takes my hand.

"Livia Mays, my love, my wife, and the mother of my child, will you dance with me?"

Tears spring into my eyes as I nod.

When he takes me into his arms this time, it's not

just him and me dancing our waltz. It's also our baby, tucked between us, the unexpected surprise that has blessed us.

And as we circle the stage area, carefully staying within the range of lights and cameras like the professionals we are, I know all the things I've learned in my years with Blitz will help us through the days ahead. The lawsuit doesn't matter. Our careers don't matter. This is what counts. Him. Me. Our baby.

One unit, together, protected and loved.

B litz and I stay for a set of questions and answers from Blaine on camera, and then escape out of Bennett's office building.

We're running out the door when we realize neither of us has a car. Juliet brought me to the building, and Bennett brought Blitz.

We stand there flummoxed in the warm summer sunshine, then burst out laughing.

"Should I call an Uber?" Blitz asks.

"I guess we could hitchhike." I lift up my skirt to show my knee.

The whole situation strikes us as outrageously funny.

"I've only been a dad for half an hour and already I've gotten us stranded on a street corner," Blitz says.

Bennett's office is tucked away on the backside of

the quiet street in San Antonio's rather modest north side. We can't stay here for long, though, or someone will recognize us.

We duck back into the shade of the building.

"I guess we shouldn't have ditched our rides," I say. We had literally waltzed our way out of the room.

But we should have known Bennett would think of everything. A sleek black Mercedes pulls up to the curb. The front passenger window rolls down, and a uniformed man I recognize as one of the Claremont drivers leans over.

"Mr. Craven? Ms. Mays? Mr. Claremont thought you might be in need of a ride."

And just in time. A group of young women exits the building, talking excitedly that they had heard Blitz was in the building.

"There he is!" one cries, and they all dig out their cell phones.

The driver jumps out, but Blitz is already opening the back door. "Ladies first," he says and I duck inside.

The driver realizes we're already in and hurries back to his seat. A trio of cell phones records our departure.

"That's just a taste of what tomorrow is going to look like." Blitz leans back and rests his head on the seat.

"Nothing we're not used to."

"I don't think it's sunk in yet. I'm going to be a dad."

I take his hand and lift it to my lips. "Are you okay with what I did?"

I never would've brought this up in front of the cameras. But I can now. "I got a heck of a lot of money to sell this. I thought it might help us until the lawsuit is taken care of, in case it goes on forever."

Blitz draws me closer. "I think it was amazing. How many people have a whole professional crew recording one of the biggest moments of their lives?"

I laugh. "I guess we did cheat them out of a wedding. So we gave them this."

"On our own terms," Blitz adds.

"Exactly," I say. "I don't mind selling our souls when I'm the one who benefits."

Blitz plants a kiss on my temple. "I knew you'd see the light."

"I had to pay for baby shoes somehow."

"About that," he says. "I'm supposed to shoot a pilot of the new dance show in about four weeks. But now I don't want to leave you."

"I can go with you."

"Can you fly when you're pregnant?"

"I have no idea. I was on house arrest last time. But I think so, right up until the end. They only stop you when you might go into labor at any moment."

"We can check with the doctors. Even so, we could always make a road trip of it."

"And you can stop at every McDonald's on the way."

"Now you're talking. I can't wait to indoctrinate this one in the ways of the Happy Meal." He pats my belly.

"I guess we should hole up," I say. "The news will break tomorrow morning. But before that, we should visit my mom and your parents to make sure they hear the news from us."

"Good thinking," Blitz says. "If my mother learned about this from a tweet, she would never forgive me."

"Let me call my mom," I say. "Maybe we can even stop by Dreamcatcher and let Danika and the teachers know. When we get to your parents, it will probably be an entire evening, so let's save them for last."

Blitz kisses my knuckles, his eyes alight with happiness. "As always, you've planned it all out."

"I had a lot of help."

"You're going to be the perfect mother."

He settles me into the seat beside him. I can almost see his happy glow.

This has been amazing.

MY MOTHER SUGGESTS WE MEET AT THE DANCE academy since it's only a few blocks from our house, and that would get her and my brother away from my father.

I'm not sure how he'll react to the news that I'm pregnant again. I'm married this time, and it should be a joyful thing. But with him, I never know. We've only shared a handful of words since I left home. If getting married didn't bridge that gap, I'm not sure anything ever will.

Blitz and I walk down the hall lined with dance studios, pausing outside the window to watch the young ballerinas in the *Dance of the Shades* room. It's where Blitz and I met for the first time, and where he taught me to waltz.

So many of our important firsts happened within these walls. It is probably my favorite place in the world to be.

My friend Suze, who runs the front desk, finds us sitting on a bench. My mom and brother are behind her.

"It's so good to see you," Mom says with a tight hug. "I feel like it's been forever."

Blitz lifts my little brother, Andy, and flips him upside down. Andy argues, "Come on Blitz, I'm too old for that."

And he's right. My baby brother is growing up.

He's eleven now, and I'm already starting to wonder where the years have gone.

Mom sits next to me on the bench. "You look a little tired," mom says, brushing hair away from my face.

"I am a little," I say.

"Something big happening?" she asks, and I wonder if she sees it. She knew last time, she saw how hard pregnancy had been.

Several of the mothers waiting on their children turn their heads. Of course, they are listening. We're lucky they're not taking pictures. We don't come to Dreamcatcher as often as we used to, so the new parents don't know us as well and treat us like celebrities, not fellow dancers.

"We can go to Danika's office," Suze says.

"Let's do," I say. Blitz and I walk hand-in-hand as we lead our party through the foyer and over to the private offices.

Danika stands from behind her desk when we arrive. "I heard you were here!" she says. She comes around to envelop me in a hug. Her hair is still blue after all these years. I can never see her any other way.

Suze closes the door.

"We have news," I say. "It's going to hit all the entertainment sites tomorrow, but we wanted it to come directly from us first."

The door opens a crack. It's Jacob and Aurora.

"Class just let out," Aurora says. "We wanted to catch you!"

More hugs. I wonder if we'll ever get the news out.

The room is crowded.

"Just say your news!" Andy says, exasperated.

"So impatient," I tease, ruffling his hair. "Blitz and I are expecting a baby."

"What?" My brother shouts. "A baby!"

My mother lets out a sharp, "Oh!" Her gaze shifts along my body to rest on my belly.

"It's super early," I say. "I'm due in March."

The room erupts. More hugs. Mom's eyes are full of tears. I know she's thinking of last time, the granddaughter she didn't get to keep.

When Suze, Jacob, and Aurora have run back out, Danika asks, "When are you going to tell Gwen?"

I glance at Blitz. We know we will have to approach this carefully with my daughter's adoptive mother. We've agreed I can continue to see Gabriella's recitals and speak to her occasionally as long as we don't reveal I am her mother. She'll be a sister now, but she won't know.

"I'll send her a quick note assuring her this doesn't change anything," I say.

Danika nods. "Well, it's wonderful news. I guess you won't be doing any ballet troops for a while!"

"No," I say. "But Blitz is shooting a kid dance show pilot, so we'll be busy."

The conversation continues about the show, and whether the academy has any kids Blitz could fast track to the auditions.

My mom leans in. "You feeling okay?"

I nod. "It's emotional. But I'm all right."

She squeezes my arm. "You're strong. You can do this."

I hope she's right.

Chapter Nine

When we get to Blitz's parents' house, Renata is cooking something intensely flavored with peppers. We aren't inside thirty seconds before I dash to the back to throw up in the bathroom.

I'm grateful I've made it this far into the day without being sick. There will be no viral memes of me throwing up, at least not yet. If I go out in public too often, though, it's bound to happen. It doesn't last forever. I remember that. Perhaps I can stick close to home until it settles.

Wherever home is going to be for a while. The Claremont's, I suppose.

When I return to the living room where David watches television, Renata sits talking quietly on the sofa with Blitz.

David glances up at me and says, "So when are you going to fess up about the kid you're carrying?"

I can't hide my astonishment. "When did you know?"

"Of course we didn't *know*," Renata said, but I can tell she did. "David and I were just speculating because you suddenly seemed so subdued."

"Subdued. Ha," David snorts. "She's been puking her guts up since that party."

Blitz shakes his head as if he can't believe he missed it. "Well, the news will be out tomorrow morning. We just did an interview about it."

"It's perfectly lovely," Renata says. "Maybe I should take up knitting."

"You do whatever your grandma's heart desires," Blitz says, patting his mother's hand.

The ever-present kitchen timer goes off in the other room. I anticipate the next wave of nausea when Renata takes out whatever savory dish she's cooking, and suggest to Blitz that maybe we should head back to the Claremont estate.

"You're not going to stay here?" Renata asks.

"It'll be a publicity storm tomorrow, Mom," Blitz says. "We should ride it out someplace with security."

"I see," she says. "I guess we should count ourselves lucky they've never been too interested in us."

David grunts in the corner.

"Let me know if anybody starts stalking this street, and I'll send someone out to help." He kisses his mom on the forehead. "I'd go catch that casserole before it burns."

My white car is parked in the garage, so we take it over to the Claremont's. I'm lucky we have someone like Bennett and Juliet to hide us away for the oncoming storm.

Bennett told Blitz that he and Juliet would be out late that night and not to expect them at dinner, so we have a quiet meal on the back patio. Our conversations are like nothing we've ever had before. Baby names. Plans for a house. Where we should live to keep our privacy.

Blitz isn't sure he wants to do the talent show now. "Shouldn't we try to stay out of the limelight, at least for a couple of years?"

I shrug. "It seems like these are the years when it's easiest for you to travel and work. There isn't a lot the paparazzi can do to a baby."

Only us. And Gwen. I need to message her before the news hits. I can't wait to introduce Gabriella to her sibling, even if I can't tell her the baby is related to her.

"You ready to go up?" Blitz asks.

"I am."

When we reach the guest wing where I've been staying, the mansion is quiet and still.

Blitz picks me up in his arms and turns in a circle. "Well, it doesn't feel like I'm carrying two," he says.

I smack his shoulder. "The baby's the size of a grain of rice right now."

"How do you know?"

The Internet," I say.

He sets me on the bed and kneels down, his face level with my belly. "I don't guess a grain of rice has ears yet," he says. "But can I talk to her anyway?"

My eyes smart with tears. "Of course. If you start talking now, one day soon, the very first words she ever hears will be yours."

Blitz rests his head in my lap for a moment. "When will she start to kick?"

"As I recall, about the halfway mark."

"So it'll be several months before I can feel her."

"That's right."

He brushes my hair off my shoulder. "And what about the other stuff? Are there things we shouldn't do? To keep the baby safe?"

"It's fine to do all the things," I tell him. "Maybe a little gentler than usual."

He feigns indignation. "My lady, are you suggesting I am too ardent?"

A giggle escapes. "I would never besmirch your honor. But, we should be careful with my belly. It's not the baby's safety I'm worried about. I just don't want to ruin the moment by puking."

Now he laughs. "Point taken."

He raises up to plant a kiss on my temple. "I will treat you as gently as a flower."

And I do feel *in bloom* as Blitz carefully removes the blue dress. In the years we've been together, we've done this act so many ways. Passionate. Emotional. Tender. Crazy. We've done it in cars, prop rooms, suspended on silks, and even once, inside a fake volcano.

But we've never done it like this. With another life between us, cradled in my belly. Never with such tender hope. Such wonder.

Blitz feathers gentle kisses along the length of my body, taking his time across my hips and stomach. "Hello, little one," he says in singsong. "I know you don't mind because this is how you came to be."

He makes me smile. And as the warmth of his breath slides up to capture a breast between his lips, I arch to him. His fingers dance along my skin, making my breath increase. I'm overwhelmed with every-thing we are and will be.

Tendrils of emotion curl through me, and this act tonight is more than just an expression of love between husband and wife. It's faith, security, and love. We leave the worries behind. The lawsuit. The show. The publicity storm that begins in the morning.

It's like it was in the beginning. A dancer and his

partner, and the music that communicates how we feel.

When his body enters mine, it's a connection like no other. My breath sucks in like it's the first time all over again, like there's never been any act before this one. With this tiny life arriving, everything is new. And at the same time, everything is as it always has been, and I pray, as it always will be.

Chapter Ten

B litz and I wake to the relentless ding of both our phones. We have most notifications turned off, naturally, as hits on us on social media would drain our phones in an hour. These are just from people we know.

Blitz rolls over to snuggle his head into my neck. "Mo-om, five more minutes."

"You going to call me Mom now?" I'm amused by this.

"You can call me your daddy."

"Blitz!" I elbow him in the gut.

He snuggles closer. "You know you like it."

"Blitz!" I say again. "Give me your phone. Let's see what everyone's saying."

"That you're a goddess, and I've been voted most likely to be a deadbeat dad."

"Hush." I roll over him to grab my phone.

But I've forgotten something important.

My morning crackers.

My stomach roils. "Never mind." I scramble over him to lunge for the bathroom door.

I've been careful leading up to the reveal to minimize my sickness in front of him. Apparently, it all went out the window the moment we were done.

The echo of my retching seems loud, and I wish I'd shut myself in.

Blitz stands in the doorway. "You okay, baby?"

I can't answer. I have nothing in my stomach so early, and everything is acrid and vile. It burns, and I hate Blitz seeing me like this. But there's nothing I can do.

Blitz grabs a washcloth and runs it under the faucet. My stomach heaves again, but there's nothing to come out. Blitz presses the cool cloth to my forehead, smoothing my hair away. "I'm so sorry," he says.

I think it's finally run its course, so I flush the toilet and lay my head on my arms. Blitz moves the cloth to the back of my neck.

"I guess being this sick is normal?" he asks quietly.

I nod, still not looking up. While it's nice to have someone with me when I'm sick, unlike my teenage pregnancy when I faced everything alone, it's also mortifying.

I need to rinse my mouth, find my voice again. But for a moment I just sit there, my knees on the cold tile floor, the long T-shirt I'm wearing bunched up at my waist. I feel a long way from my glamorous ballerina career, or the photo shoot yesterday.

After a few minutes, it seems safe enough to pull away from the toilet. "Give me a second to clean up," I rasp out.

Blitz leaves the room so I can wash my face and brush my teeth and feel somewhat human again. It's so early in this pregnancy that I can't yet see the light at the end of the morning sickness tunnel.

When I return to the bedroom, Blitz has figured out how to project our phone data onto the large television screen on the wall of the room. A Twitter feed rushes by, rolling so fast I can't even read everything.

"What's the hashtag?" I ask.

"There are several," Blitz says. "The morning show didn't provide one, and it doesn't look like our social media team is on the ball for this."

"I should have alerted them to what I was going to do," I say. "That was a big oversight."

Blitz shrugs. "Sometimes the best ones come naturally by the fans."

"Is anything trending?"

"It looks like the simplest one. #blitzbaby."

I nod. "That's what I would've picked."

We watch the mentions scroll by for a few minutes, and then Blitz turns to the notifications from people we know. There are lots of congratulations from the *Dance Blitz* staff, several other celebrities who have Blitz's contact information, and one from Shelly, his personal assistant. There's even one from Hannah, Blitz's old agent. He fired her, but she still represents him for anything related to the old dance show, per her ironclad contract.

When I see it, I ask, "You won't have to keep Hannah as the agent for the new talent show, will you?"

"No way. She only gets a percentage of anything branded with *Dance Blitz*. The new show will be a completely new brand."

I sit on the edge of the bed. Some of the former contestants have started tweeting, and the retweets of their messages are getting lots of hits.

"Oh, look, our dear friend Giselle wishes us well with the baby." Blitz pauses the feed.

"Didn't we have Twitter block her ability to tag you?"

"She didn't tag. But she can participate in any of the hashtags."

We'll never shake that woman. As long as her career is not as successful as she hopes, she will continue to try to ride on Blitz's fame.

"Everything looks positive overall," Blitz says. He

scrolls through his messages until he finds one from the social media team. "Okay, here's an update from Karina. They're watching for any negative spin. They will contain it. Shelly is working with them."

I look over his shoulder at the phone. "Who's paying these people? Isn't the whole *Dance Blitz* team dismantled?"

"Technically, they work for Hannah. I guess at some point they will no longer manage anything for me. Or maybe Hannah will continue to pay them to make sure her percentage of any residuals remains as solid as possible."

"That makes sense." There's still so much about this business I have to learn.

"Did you have any ideas for how you wanted to handle the news beyond giving Blaine the scoop?"

"Bennett has some things in the pipeline," I say. "Several online shops will produce everything from T-shirts to baby bibs. He has a team to insert themselves in the hashtags and start advertising, and we get a percentage."

"Always thinking, that's my girl." He plants a kiss on my hair. "What shall we do in exile?"

"My baby daddy is going to go fetch me some plain toast and orange juice to see if I can get anything down without throwing up."

He stands up and gives me a salute. He looks so charming in nothing but a pair of boxers, his hair all tousled. This is the Blitz only I get to see. And I will never forget I am lucky.

He digs around in his duffel bag for a shirt. "So when do I get to start fetching watermelon in the middle of winter, and mustard and pickle sandwiches?"

I lie back on the bed. "I don't know. I didn't have anyone to fetch these things last time, so if I craved anything weird, I just ignored it."

Blitz lies down beside me again. "Will you have a lot of negative flashbacks to your pregnancy with Gabriella as this goes on? I think trauma often gets revisited."

"I already am," I say. "But I can handle it. Everything is so different this time."

"You messaged Gwen, right?"

"I did. I didn't hear back, but at least she heard the news from me."

"Maybe one day she'll let Gabriella in on the secret."

"I can't count on that."

"Well, I'm here for whatever you need," Blitz says. He hops back up to head to the kitchen. "I'm hoping that will occasionally be a Big Mac and fries."

I shake my head. "Don't count on it, fry guy."

He gives me a huge grin and heads out into the hall.

The sun filtering through the leaves of the trees

outside the window leaves a lacey pattern on the ceiling. I feel better now that everyone knows the situation. I no longer have to hide.

For the last seven days, even though I knew I was doing it for a reason, secretly being pregnant felt too much like my old shame. From now on, I want my life and my family to be out in the big wide open, with all the love and attention they deserve.

Chapter Eleven

B y the time we arrive at our first official doctor
appointment, the publicity tide has definitely
turned against the producers who were suing us.

While Blitz and I absolutely cannot speak out
about the suit as we negotiate with the producers
about settling out of court before an appeal, the
social media team subtly brings about an outcry.

A new hashtag emerges. #saveblitzbaby

No one has truly leaked the financial hardship
we'll be in should the ruling stand. But no one has
corrected the huge numbers that have been thrown
around on the talk shows, amounts way beyond what
the *Dance Blitz* franchise is worth.

We're ushered to a private office through a back
door to avoid being seen by other patients. While we
wait, Blitz and I sort through the current tweets.

Blitz turns his phone to me. "This one's offering to pay our doctor bill if they don't drop the suit."

"That's sweet." Bennett's prediction that some of them might invent viral-worthy gossip hasn't happened so far.

A woman with a head of closed-shaved hair pops her head in. "We have an exam room ready for you. I'm sorry we had to shove you in here. We don't get many celebrity couples."

Blitz lowers his ball cap and keeps his sunglasses in place as we walk the hall. With our names and faces constantly trending, anybody in this office would be tempted to take a quick photo of us and tweet our location.

The woman hands me a cotton gown. "Open to the back. Everything off. Dr. Schneider will be doing a transvaginal sonogram. Have you had one before?"

I nod. The memory of it rises up, my glowering father refusing to leave the room. My mom's trembling hands. Everything had been done in one visit. Confirming I was indeed pregnant. The sonogram to tell me how far along I was. I had been sick and crying and wanted to somehow just escape.

My thoughts must have shown on my face, because as soon as the nurse closes the door, Blitz asks, "You okay, Livia?"

"Just remembering."

He wraps his arms around me. "This is our time. And it's the happiest time."

I nod against his shoulder. I don't know how to explain it to him. This feeling is everything at once. Wonderful. Magical. And yet, full of regret. There was so little that sustained me the first time. And no matter how amazing my circumstances are the second time around, everything about this place, the white paper on the table, the silver stirrups, and the smells of antiseptic and cleaners take me back to the horror of when I was fifteen years old.

Despite these hard thoughts, I say, "I'll be fine." I pull away and hold up the cotton gown. "I think you should take a picture of me in this for the feed later. We should try to stay trending until they greenlight the pilot because you're too popular not to."

Blitz's smile is dazzling. "I never dreamed my wife would be so good at nailing media angles. What did I do to deserve you?"

I patted my belly. "Apparently you knew how to make our relationship permanent."

I switch to the cotton gown, and we take a hilarious set of dramatic photographs and selfies inside the room for the social media team to review. With the pilot shooting next week, Shelly has already moved the best players from the old team to the new one in hopes of keeping everyone's attention as we negotiate a deal.

I'm fighting for our future, as entertainers, as parents, but most of all, as a couple who control their own fate. I will not let heavy-handed producers from a show built on Blitz's charisma derail our lives any longer.

With all the time we spent taking pictures, I've barely sat down on the exam table when Dr. Schneider walks in. He's tall and gangly, his gray hair thick and curly.

"I get to deliver the most famous baby in all of Texas," he says. "Are you ready to take a look?"

"We are," Blitz says, rubbing his hands together. "Will we get a copy of this?"

"Absolutely. It might be my most famous work."

The young female nurse who comes in this time has stars in her eyes. She keeps touching her phone, and I think she's dying to take our picture.

Blitz must be reading my thoughts as I watch the nurse, because he says, "I guess you talked to the staff about not revealing our coming here? Because if word gets out, you're going to have a security problem even when we're not here. They'll camp out hoping to see us."

Dr. Schneider helps me lie back on the pillow. "Everyone's been briefed."

Blitz takes my hand as Dr. Schneider presses on my belly. "Uterus feels good and firm, about the right size. All seems well here."

He nods at the nurse, who rolls up a sonogram machine. "Let's take some measurements and get a peek at that heartbeat." He sits down and types on the machine. "What was your last menstrual period date?"

I tell him and he taps in a few more characters. "This gives you a due date of March 7. Let's see if junior measures up."

He turns the screen so we can all see it and squirts a hefty amount of clear jelly on the sonogram wand.

Blitz is fascinated by everything. "That looks like a jazzy space microphone," he says.

The nurse bursts out laughing, and then covers her mouth. I'm sure she's already relating the story to her friends. We'll be lucky if this doesn't get out.

Dr. Schneider pushes the paper drape higher, and I feel the wand sliding up against me.

The familiar collection of white blips showers across the black screen.

"What is this?" Blitz asks. "I can't make anything out."

Dr. Schneider continues to move the wand around until he gets the view he's looking for. "Livia is a little more than eight weeks along," he says. "Some people call this the peanut stage. Here is the baby." His finger points out the shape on the screen. "I'm going to measure how long the baby is." He moves the lines. A number pops up. *8 weeks 1 day*. "Right on the money. Exactly the right size for what we predicted."

"Is she okay?" Blitz asks. His face is tight with concern.

Dr. Schneider holds the wand still and turns a dial on the machine. A *whomp, whomp, whomp* sound fills the room.

"That's the baby's heartbeat."

Blitz stands up and looks closer. My eyes smart with tears. There she is. Or he. The tiny pulse of the heartbeat brightens and shifts, a plus sign marking it.

"That's her, isn't it?" Blitz makes a fist and presses it to his lips. I've never seen him like this. I glance from the screen to his face and back. Our baby. It's just become real to him.

He turns to me. "That's our baby." He presses his forehead against mine. "She's right there."

"She is."

The moment lingers, and it's definitely nothing like I've ever known. The sound of the heartbeat, the love we feel pulsing with each sound. The flow of emotion between us.

I may have had a baby before. But I have never felt such wonder and joy.

Chapter Twelve

It's safe to say my relationship with Blitz won't be the same after seeing our baby's heartbeat. Even more so than telling him I'm pregnant, this visual confirmation that his child exists makes Blitz more introspective. He listens to people rather than talks at them. He becomes more understanding.

The way he's treated me all along is now how he acts around others as well.

He's even made up with his horrid ex-agent Hannah, although he doesn't go so far as to sign with her again.

The flight to L.A. is uneventful, although I do throw up twice in the first class lavatory thanks to someone's extraordinarily strong smelling perfume.

I'm relieved to discover the location of the new kid dance show is not at the same studio as *Dance*

Blitz. As nostalgic as I could get walking down the halls of that production, I feel it's best we put our past behind us and look to our future. And this show is exactly what we need.

Drake Adler is the co-producer along with Blitz. The other two producers of *Dance Blitz* are only signed on in the capacity that calls off the lawsuit but doesn't give them enough of a stake for them to have any power over the production.

The opening pilot is a mix of acts hoping to be chosen for the main show, not unlike how other talent shows are structured. Some of the kids are incredible, and some are there more for comedic effect.

Unlike the other talent shows, though, there is no panel of judges critiquing the kids or giving them some sort of golden pass onto the show. Blitz himself works with the children to improve their acts, and their willingness to be led by him, as well as their on-stage chemistry, is a big part of who will get chosen.

It is exciting to see some of the old *Dance Blitz* staff brought back on, including my favorite hair designer Cecilia. Shelly has even tracked down Jessie, my original personal assistant.

I have no official role in this show, although I do spend some time corralling the kids in the stage wings. Some of them start calling me Mama Livia, which I take as a great honor.

A few of the acts are clear winners for the potential show. A pair of twin boys have an uncanny way of dancing exactly in sync despite only being six years old.

One ten-year-old girl, as beautiful and serene as a queen, tap dances with astonishing speed in an elaborate medieval princess costume.

A sibling set makes the studio audience gasp as they perform crazy feats of acrobatics.

I love everything about the show. The set design, the costumes, the format, but most of all, I love how my husband kneels down to get on the same level as the kids and listens to their every word. He hugs a girl who cries when she falls on a turn and hurts her ankle. He high-fives the boys who pull off a perfect break dancing routine.

The show is nothing like his old Blitz days. There is no infighting, no angst, no outrageous behavior to steal the camera's attention. It's just him, being honest and helpful and funny with the talented group.

When the lights go down, we all know this show is going to happen. The magic lingers in the air, and the kids all start cheering. They are having a blast. So are we. It's one of those moments when you know you're watching television at its best.

I hurry out onto the stage. The kids toss the remnants of confetti that dropped as Blitz brought them out for their bows. Blitz pulls me against him, smiling at the children—the tap dancing princess, the synchronized twins, and most especially, a sweet ballerina with dark hair who fills us with wonder and anticipation about who our child might become.

Blitz is already a father figure and very soon, he'll be a father.

The best really is yet to come.

Epilogue

❧❦❧

Light streams through the hospital window as the sun peeps over the horizon.

Blitz is out cold on the pullout sofa beneath it. It was a long night, for sure. He didn't even wake when the nurse came to check on me and the baby, taking her out of the clear bassinet and helping me latch her for her second official meal.

The sight of her takes my breath away. I can't stop looking. She's exactly like Gabriella, or else the short memory of my first daughter in my arms has begun to morph with this new vision. Sometimes my eyes smart sharply when I think of all these wondrous moments I never got to have with my firstborn.

It's impossible not to think of this. I'm at a different hospital, but the set up is much the same. Mom and Renata were here until around midnight, through the birth, when they took the baby for her clean up, and when they brought her back. I expect to see them again, plus my brother Andy and Blitz's father David, in a few hours. I do not expect my father to come. I'm not sure I want him.

But for right now, it's just me and Valentina Marie, downy haired, pink-faced, and quiet. Her tiny fist rests on the swell of my outrageously veiny boob.

The baby falls asleep without doing much at all by way of eating, but I've been told this will likely be the case today and probably tomorrow as well. We'll work on her latch while I'm here, then I can consult with a lactation nurse if I need more help.

This is the sum total of my worries at the moment.

The first season of Blitz's new show has been recorded and begins airing in a month. He's on hiatus as they wait to see if they are renewed. The lawsuit is over, ended when the new contracts were signed.

We bought a house.

Life is good.

The baby wriggles against me, tantalizingly close to the milk but not sure how to get it. I shift her, but this makes her more upset. Her tiny newborn cry stirs Blitz from sleep. He rolls off the bed and stumbles over.

"Everything okay?"

"Just working on positioning," I say and adjust

Valentina again. This time, her tiny mouth finds what she's looking for. But before she can get going, she's off to dreamland again.

"Must be quite a workout," Blitz says with a yawn.

"Seems like it."

We've agreed not to let the word get out about her birth until we're safely home and can control security. Since our due date was reported to be March 7 but it's only the third, the intensity of the baby watch hasn't ramped up.

Blitz pads off to the bathroom. Someone knocks at the door, and I shift my gown to cover myself since the baby isn't trying to eat right now anyway.

"Come in," I call.

I expect someone from the dance academy, or maybe Bennett and Juliet.

But my breath catches when Gwen pokes her head in. "Hey," she says. "You taking visitors? I know it's early but Gabriella goes to camp at eight."

"We've been up half the night," I say. "It's all the same to us." My voice is calm but my heart races. Why is she here? We'd only spoken once or twice since I wrote to let her know I was pregnant. Of course, she was on the short list to get the news yesterday when I went into labor.

"I bet," she says and turns to the hall. "Come on, Gabby."

Gwen holds the door as Gabriella rolls inside. She

wears a neon yellow "Camp Vision" T-shirt and a matching bow in her hair.

"You had a baby, Miss Livia!" she says. "I wanted to bring her a present."

I try mightily to hold in the sobs trying to force themselves out. My voice shakes as I say, "That's very sweet."

Gwen holds herself stiffly, but I can see her eyes are wet, too. I know this is hard for her. It's scary. But I will not tell the secret. She raised my baby when my family forced me to give her up. And she has not cut me from their lives. I will accept all her decisions and do whatever makes sense to her.

Gabriella rolls her wheelchair up to the bed and holds out a ribbon stick, pink and sparkly with a light-up heart on the end and a long tail of white ribbons. "Just like you got us a long time ago."

"I remember." I accept the stick and lay it next to the baby.

"What's her name?" Gabriella asks.

"Valentina."

"That's pretty."

Blitz comes out of the bathroom. "Oh, hey!" he says, and rounds the bed to give Gabriella a hug. "My best and favorite dancer!"

Gabriella's face blooms pink. She always did have a soft spot for him. "Hi, Blitz."

"You think we're going to teach this one to be as good as you?" he asks.

She giggles. "Maybe."

He turns to Gwen. "Glad you could come by."

Gwen gives him a small nod.

"Would you like to hold her?" I ask.

Gabriella looks up at Gwen. "Can I, Mom?"

Gwen bites her lip. "Sure, baby. Be real careful."

Blitz takes Valentina and sets her carefully in Gabriella's lap. I know it's on the tip of his tongue to say, "Here's your big sister," but he doesn't and neither do I. It's not for us to decide what she knows. Gwen is her mother.

"Let me take a picture," Blitz says, pulling his phone out of his shorts. "I'll send it to your mom."

Gabriella smiles up at him and the resemblance between her and the baby takes my breath away.

"You know," Blitz says, "You're about to have a birthday, aren't you?"

"March 12," Gabriella says. She fingers the tiny hat, and I remember the matching one I hid under my bed so long, the one that fell off in the hospital the first time around, right as the nurse took Gabriella away. Tears spill down my face and I hastily wipe them away before anyone notices.

"I think since you have a March birthday and Valentina has a March birthday, you should be special birthday friends. Maybe each year, we can have a

DEANNA ROY

March party for you and Valentina and you can celebrate together. You can show her the ropes. Someone
has to teach her how to hit a piñata."

"That's funny," Gabriella says. "Everybody knows
how to hit a piñata."

"She doesn't yet."

The baby stirs, and Blitz picks her up before she
can cry. "Deal?"

"Can we get new ribbon sticks?" Gabriella asks.

"Definitely," Blitz says.

"Then deal," she says.

I glance over at Gwen to see how she's taking this
conversation. She gives me a brief nod. "We should
get going, Gabby. We don't want to be late."

"Okay." Gabriella backs up her chair. "Bye, Livia,
bye, Blitz. She pats the baby's head. Bye, Valentina."

When the door has closed behind them, I can't
stop my crying. Blitz shifts the baby to one arm and
grabs a tissue box to pass to me. "You're okay, Mama,"
he says. "Your girls got to see each other."

I can't do anything but pull tissues from the box
and press them to my eyes.

"It's a good sign," Blitz goes on. "If Gwen brought
her today, that means she's open to seeing her outside
the dance studio."

I nod behind my cloud of Kleenex. He's right. I'm
grateful.

Valentina makes another tiny cry, and I hold out

my arms. We'll try this latch again. And in a little while, the family will descend. Then our friends. Then our fans will find out.

We are surrounded by love. We have each other.

And at least once a year, my two girls will get to celebrate together. Blitz's quick thinking made that happen.

When Valentina is actually latched and trying to eat, I hold out my hand. "Give me your phone," I say.

He knows what I'm after and pulls up the image he took.

I gaze at it while the baby curls her tiny hand against my skin. My two girls. "You got to meet your sister," I whisper, knowing it's one of the few times in Valentina's life I will get to say it out loud. "And she loved you."

Blitz sits next to me on the bed, arranging my hair so it stays out of the baby's way. He leans down to kiss my head and we stay this way a while. Life will move forward soon, and oftentimes it will feel out of control.

But at each milestone, each fork in the road, we will make our decisions the best we can, and march solidly on. Together. United. In honesty, openness, and always, in love.

THANK YOU FOR READING THE ENTIRE DANCE Series! After we adopted our little boy, I knew I would begin incorporating the complexity of adoption into some of my stories. There are so many layers — the birth mom, the adoptive mom, the children, their half-siblings. I will be exploring this idea even more in future books.

Did you read the prequel to the Dance books? Before Livia and Blitz met, before Dreamcatcher Dance Academy was even built, there was the story of Bennett and Juliet Claremont.

Juliet is born on the Claremont estate to her dance instructor mother. She falls in love with not one, but TWO Claremont brothers. Don't miss her story of how she sorts it out in Billionaire's Dance.

Also by Deanna Roy

The Forever Series

A young couple reunites in college, four years after the death of their newborn.

- Forever Innocent (Corabelle & Gavin)
- Forever Loved (Corabelle & Gavin)
- Forever Sheltered (Tina & Darion)
- Forever Bound (Jenny & Chance)
- Forever Family (Corabelle, Tina, Jenny)
- Forever Christmas (Corabelle & Gavin)

- Boxed Set: First Three Books
- Boxed Set: Final Three Books

- Stella and Dane (Standalone)

The Lovers Dance Series

A sheltered ballerina is lured into the life of a brash TV reality show star.

- Forbidden Dance
- Wounded Dance
- Wicked Dance
- Tender Dance
- Final Dance

- Lovers Dance Boxed Set

- Billionaire's Dance (a standalone prequel)

Other Books

- Conversations with Little Dude
  (Nonfiction stories with her son who was adopted from foster care)

- In the Company of Angels (A fill-in-the-pages baby record book for babies lost to miscarriage or stillbirth)
- The Magic Mayhem trilogy of action/adventure books for children ages 9-12.

Small town feel-good romance

Don't miss Deanna's pen name Abby Tyler. As Abby, Deanna writes funny, feel-good small-town romances with a recurring cast of feisty senior citizens and the couples they push together, by hook or by crook.

Deanna is the six-time *USA Today* bestselling author of romance and women's fiction.

She is a passionate advocate for women who have miscarried. She founded the web site Pregnancy-Loss.info in 1998 after the loss of her first baby and continues to run both online and in-person support groups for women who have endured this impossible loss.

She is a foster mom, an adoptive mom, and a baby loss mom. She lives in Austin, Texas, with her family.

Learn more about the author at
www.deannaroy.com

Join her email or text list for new release notices at
Deanna's List

facebook.com/deannaroyauthor

twitter.com/deannaroy

instagram.com/deannaroyauthor

goodreads.com/Goodreads

bookbub.com/authors/deanna-roy

Sneak Peek of Billionaire's Dance

The front doors of the estate flew open. A butler I had never seen before hurried out.

"I am so sorry, Miss Parker. We weren't expecting you for another two hours. Did you take a taxi? We could have sent a car for you." He hurriedly motioned to a young man I didn't know to retrieve my bags.

"Oh!" I said. "I think there has been a mistake. I —"

I stopped short when Quinn appeared on the

front porch in tennis gear. He rested a racket on his shoulder. "You're awfully dressed up for a tennis pro."

My voice didn't seem to work as I took him in. I was already flustered and not ready to see him yet. He was twenty-seven now, tan and muscled in the fitted shirt over loose shorts.

"Miss Parker, I'll escort you to your guesthouse," the butler said. "Would you like a golf cart to take you around?"

My lips were frozen. Quinn was staring right at me, but he didn't see me for who I was, the awkward teen who'd been his friend as a girl.

Should I try to pull this off? Tennis pro? He obviously didn't know this instructor very well. Maybe I resembled her picture.

I stood up straight, tugging on the bottom of the smart fitted jacket to my suit. We looked at each other, and I could see the interest in his eyes. His gaze raked over my tawny gold jacket and matching skirt, down my legs to the achingly high Louboutins.

"Won't you come in for a quick drink before we hit the nets?" Quinn gestured to his outfit. "I had planned to lob a few balls before you arrived, but perhaps we could talk strategy first. Over some champagne? Or would that ruin our training regimen?"

I still couldn't speak. My heart hammered. He held out his hand to me. I itched to take it. It's what I'd always wanted.

The young man stood with my bags, waiting on my order. I could go in, see the ruse through. I wouldn't get far. The cook would spot me. Or one of the girls. Although if Quinn couldn't see it...

"Miss Parker?" the butler asked.

I was about to admit who I was when a glossy black Mercedes pulled up to the circle drive. Probably the real Miss Parker, and I was about to be outed.

I turned around, trying to decide if I should admit who I was or just let it happen.

But the driver was Bennett, Quinn's older brother.

"Oh, it's the boring brother," Quinn said. "Let's hurry before he spoils all the fun. I'll tell you straight out, he was not thrilled about my idea of bringing a tennis pro out full-time."

Quinn had always disparaged Bennett's seriousness, but back then it was always playful. Now his words had an edge to them.

My voice didn't want to work, and the explanation about who I was stuck in my throat. The moments hurtled by as Bennett stepped out of the car.

Quinn moved from the doorway to stand beside me. I turned to him, thinking surely now that he was close he would see who I was.

If only I could keep up this ruse a little longer!

Bennett headed up the steps. He nodded to the

butler. "Hello, Adams," he said to him. He glanced at me. "Hello, Juliet. Nice to have you back after so long."

Then he went inside.

My face blasted hot. He knew me! Now what would happen?

Quinn's head snapped around. "Juliet?"

I was so busted.

Go back to before Dreamcatcher's Dance Academy was founded, when Juliet had to choose between Quinn, the billionaire brother she has loved since childhood, and his brother Bennett in Billionaire's Dance.